REDEEMED

Redeemed

THE SOULMATES SERIES

BOOK 3

LIV RANCOURT

This is a work of fiction. Names, characters, places, businesses and incidents either are the product of the author's imagination or are used fictitiously. Any resemblance to actual persons, living or dead, events, or locales is entirely coincidental.

Soulmates
© 2020 by Amy Dunn Caldwell

Cover Art: Amy Caldwell
Editor: Meg DesCamp

ISBN-13: 978-1-7368520-6-4

This book is dedicated to families – bio or found, those we were born into or those we create. No one should have to fly solo.

TABLE OF CONTENTS

GLOSSARY

Ádh mór balbh - good luck, dumbass
Affaire du cœur — love affair
Amore mio — my love
An marbhdhraoi — a necromancer
Beurteilung — *assessment* - werewolf term
for resolving conflict with a fight to death
Dia á sábháil — Oh my God
Meascach — halfbreed
Mo bhanríon — my queen
Mo chath — my battle
Mo chontúirt — my perils
Mo leannáin — my lovers
Mo mhuirnin — my dear, my darling
Mo rúndiamhra — my mysteries
Mo rúin — my secrets
Mo shíorghrá — my soulmate
Tá mé ag siúl fear marbh.- Dead man walking

PART ONE: NO MURDER. NO WAY

CHAPTER ONE

DAVID

Check it. We're in a Ralph's parking lot near the corner of Obama Boulevard and S. La Brea, and I'm ready to start knocking heads together. Connor wants to call the car rental company and extend our contract for another day. I don't know why we're renting cars when it'd be more anonymous to use Uber. Trajan sees nothing wrong with *borrowing* a car when we need one.

Trajan's thinking his way would be cheaper. I mean, he's not wrong, as long as we don't get arrested, an issue the vampire doesn't stop to consider. When you can *suggest* that a cop go bother someone else, *borrowing* cars is NBD.

Except our Boy Scout Boyfriend won't put up with us stealing cars on the regular.

Connor and Trajan are in the front seat of our rented Toyota, while I'm draped across the back. "Staying out of sight would be easier if we weren't in the same car all the time." I try for patience but don't really stick the landing. Trajan parked his Land Rover in Stone's warehouse for the duration, but if we keep any car for too long, Jacques will find it.

Connor glances at me with a half smirk. "Do you know how many RAV4s there are in the city of Los Angeles?"

Trajan doesn't answer him, and neither do I.

"We've got all our stuff in here already. Let's just go to wherever we're staying tonight, and I'll pay for an extra day." Connor puts the car in gear, as if he's settled the argument.

I guess he has. I mean, so what if Jacques Betancourt's minions connect us to this particular pearly grey RAV4? At least it's nicer than the last car Connor rented.

Tonight, we're staying in a VRBO off Crenshaw. The neighborhood's not Beverly Hills, but we've stayed in sketchier places. I deliberately chose a bit of an upgrade; after three weeks on the run, staying no longer than two days in any one place, I'm over the whole anonymous-hotel-room-with-smelly-carpet-and-a-vampire-closet thing.

I'm also desperate for a washer and dryer. There are only so many times I can wear the same pair of jeans.

We're lying low, while at the same time trying to figure out where Jacques is hiding. *Jacques, Jacques, Jacques*. Trajan's maker and now his curse. Jacques wants Connor dead, and he told Trajan to do the deed.

And a vampire can't really argue with his maker.

But there'll be no killing, not if I can help it. No way am I going to let our very pleasant menage break up over murder.

No fucking way.

The only sound is the GPS giving Connor directions to our new place. Trajan hasn't really said much since he rose. He's still wearing black wrap-around shades because he claimed the sun hadn't fully set when we left on this little adventure. Looks pretty damned dark to me, but I like his hitman chic vibe so I don't call him on it.

When Siri tells us our destination is on the right, I straighten in my seat. The place is white stucco and a pair of fierce looking sword plants guard either side of the front door. "If you two grab the bags, I'll bring the groceries in and start dinner," I say. "And if you're hungry too, Tray…"

I let the words fade and he hums a response. Not quite the level of enthusiasm I was hoping for, but better than nothing.

"Let's get the gear in." Connor parks in the driveway. The glance he sends my way says he might be hungrier for more than the steaks we bought, and I roll my eyes. We might be hiding from a pissed-off vampire sire, but our dicks don't really care.

Giving myself a shake, I grab the shopping bags and head for the front door. We can play when our stuff's stowed away and the SUV is in the garage. They wait in the car until I've got the door unlocked. These moments, while we hustle between whatever we're driving and wherever we're staying, feel too exposed, and my heart trips along while I punch in the code to open the lockbox holding the key.

I open the door, invite Trajan in, and head for the kitchen. Once we're inside we're safe—or safer—because Jacques' vampire minions can't come in without an invitation. Locked doors won't keep out non-vamp minions, but they'll slow them down at least.

Connor and I alternate cooking—well, one of us cooks and the other feeds Trajan. There's something fairly erotic in watching your vampire lover feed while you're grating cheese over pasta or tossing a salad.

"It's the closest thing we have to a tradition," I say, setting the Ralph's bags on the counter.

Connor leans through the kitchen door, a suitcase in each hand. "What?"

"Nah, nothing." I smile to show I'm really okay. It's a waste of time to feel bad that we don't have regular date nights while we're doing our best to stay alive.

The house is SoCal standard: one story, tile floors, white walls, dark wood. There are two bedrooms, one windowless for vampires and the other with a king-sized bed and a small bathroom attached. The images on the VRBO site looked nice enough and the fact that neither Connor nor Trajan has hit me with any complaints yet tells me all must be as advertised.

The kitchen is a big open space divided by a center island, with a dining table on one end. The table's pushed up against the wall with what looks like a church pew rather than chairs.

Not that I've spent a lot of time in churches, but it makes me want to genuflect or something.

I'm peppering the steaks when Connor and Trajan come in. Connor's got his laptop and his work face on and Trajan's wearing a forced smile.

"What's up?" I ask, flipping the steaks so I can doctor the other side.

"Not much." Connor opens his laptop, tapping the table with one finger. "I got an email from beyond the grave."

I set the shaker down with a click. "From whom?"

Trajan's too stiff and Connor's smile is grim. "Adam Smith."

"Fuuuck." Adam Smith, former supernatural liaison to the LAPD and part-time murderer, fell under the shadow of Connor's bodach form and departed for the great beyond. "What does that even mean?"

"The night we went to the cemetery I asked him if he had a list of all the vampire sires in the Los Angeles area, and he said he'd let me know."

"Wow. He takes his commitments seriously." I realize Connor and I are the only ones talking. Trajan's with us, right? "Couldn't you just have asked our in-house vampire?"

"Yeah." Connor swipes the hair back from his face with a sheepish smile. His hair is almost long enough for a ponytail and although he shaved the other day, he's back to a Miami Vice stubble. "I don't remember why I asked Smith first. The request made sense at the time."

Trajan stirs. "There's Loralie D'Ambrosio. She and her trio have lived off the old blood in Pasadena since '89."

"Is that 1889 or 1989?" My smile is the picture of innocence.

Trajan doesn't blink. "The first one."

"Do you know Roland FitzEustace, Viscount Baltinglass?" Connor asks.

That earns a snort from the vampire. "Rollie's a fucking poser."

"So, yes." Connor makes a note.

"Last I heard he and his harem were stalking Venice Beach. Jacques and Rollie have hated each other for over a hundred years, so he's probably your best bet."

I stab the steak with a fork, tenderizing it. "Best bet for what?"

"Figuring out how to break Jacques' hold over Trajan." Connor speaks low and keeps typing. The sudden upsurge in tension raises the hairs on the back of my neck.

Trajan's eyes are so dark he could be wearing those shades again. "I'm not sure it can be done."

My wolf rumbles at his words, adding heat to my verbal clapback. "Of course it can be done. You're pack. We'll figure it out."

"He's right." Connor gives Trajan a measured look and slides the laptop over so he can see it. "Tell me who else we should talk to."

Trajan's busy looking at his fingernails. "Start with Rollie, although call him Lord Baltinglass, and then look for Delia Packard. She's got this huge house right in Rolling Hills, but as far as I know only a couple of her scions are in the area. She's older than Jacques by a few years and while she probably has more children than all of them, she gives them almost complete independence. They'll come if they have to, but she rarely calls."

I heat the broiler and turn my attention to the salad. I sense Connor's exhale from across the room, but out of the corner of my eye I can see that Trajan's still sitting too stiffly. "Anybody hungry?"

Neither answer me. *Damn.* I'd been hoping for dinner-as-foreplay, but something's definitely off. Connor's absorbed in his screen and Trajan's absorbed in his own navel, as near as I can tell. I chop tomatoes and try to find a way in.

"Let me talk to them first." The words burst out of Trajan, startling me so badly I almost slice my thumb.

Connor fixes him with a hard stare. "That oughta go well."

"You know less than you think."

I feel like I've walked into a conversation that's been going on for a while.

"Come on, Tray. You can't seriously think asking a vampire sire how to break with Jacques won't have consequences."

The way Trajan shrugs reminds me of the semi-despondent guy who met me at LAX.

I set the knife down before I use it on something other than tomatoes. "Okay, here's how tonight's going to go." I rifle through drawers until I find a towel for my hands. "I'm going to text Sheena so she can keep you company while Connor and I chat up our neighborhood vamps, and then we're all going to make use of that premium king-sized bed."

There's a long silence. I keep my chin up to show I mean it.

"It's a queen," Trajan finally says.

"What?"

"In the windowless room. It's a queen-sized bed."

He's the tiniest bit more relaxed, and so am I. "I'll mention it in the review."

I slide the steaks under the broiler, leaving the oven door cracked so I can see it if they catch fire. Connor closes his laptop and for a moment I think he's going to leave the room. Instead, he slides his chair closer to Trajan's.

"Come, *mo shíorghrá*." He holds out his hand. "Feed. You need to eat."

The look they give each other is so hot the steak's not the only thing that might catch fire. My lovers reach for each other and Trajan whispers, "I will not give in to him," as he tugs Connor closer.

"I know." Connor folds himself into Trajan's lap. There's nothing childlike in his posture. Instead, the tilt of Connor's head on Trajan's shoulder shows a rare kind of trust. The vampire wraps his arms around Connor as if he's holding a precious thing. For two such powerful men, their moment of vulnerability pierces something deep in me. I want to join them, to wrap myself around them, but I hold off out of respect for their shared history.

And because I'm afraid of saying something I might later regret.

Trajan feeds and the moment passes and the steaks do not, in fact, catch fire. While Connor and I eat, Trajan tells us what he knows about Rollie FitzEustace and Delia Packard. Neither sound particularly threatening. I mean, beyond the fact that they're vampires who've each had a couple hundred years to accumulate power. And because I'm the practical sort, I spend most of the meal strategizing the correct outfit for interviewing deadly predators.

Like, something with the highest heels I can manage.

You can't just walk up to a vampire's house and knock on the door. It involves correspondence and intermediaries. More than once, Connor reaches into his pocket, presumably hoping to find the badge he'd worn as a member of the Elites.

Because membership in the supernatural FBI had its benefits.

At any rate, Trajan texted a guy who messaged Connor. After a couple of rough drafts, the three of us hit the right mix of obsequious and charming and sent a formal request. In return, an anonymous number texted Connor an invitation.

"I guess we're in," he says, shrugging into his leather jacket. The late September night isn't truly cool enough for that level of outerwear, but it's thick enough to slow down most weapons. I hope.

I settle for worn jeans that aren't entirely clean, boots with a stacked heel, and a deep purple button-down with subtle silver threaded stripes. It's a going-out top, but loose enough that if I have to shift, I can pull it off over my head without shredding it.

"That your seventies drag?" Trajan asks. He's still in one of the big wooden dining chairs, holding himself stiffly, as if he might otherwise devolve into a puddle of nervous tics.

"You love it." I scratch my belly, giving him a peek at skin.

Even his smile is careful. "Mmhmm."

"We've got an hour to get over to Venice Beach, so we better leave now." Connor glances from one of us to the other.

"Sure." I clomp across the room and give Trajan a gentle kiss on the cheek. "We should be back in a couple of hours."

He intertwines our fingers. "Sheena'll be here after The Club closes. Text us if things go bad."

"They won't."

I can't quite drum up Connor's level of confidence, but I squeeze Trajan's fingers anyway. "They won't."

My mind understands why it'd be problematic to have a vampire ask directly how to break from his maker but my heart winces at leaving Trajan alone. He might have survived on his own for much longer than I've been alive, but he's only wanted to sever his relationship with Jacques once, and the consequences of that could be dire.

Without a lot of conversation, Connor and I pile into the RAV4. He's found the garage door remote, so in short order we're getting to know our neighbors on La Cienega Boulevard. You'd think the traffic would be lighter after midnight on a Tuesday.

You'd be wrong.

Ignoring Siri's insistence that *your destination is on the left*, Connor drives past the house on our first pass. It's several blocks from the actual beach, and its white walls and red tiled roof share an architectural style with our VRBO but on a grander scale. All the lights are on and the whole place buzzes with energy.

Our message must have stirred up the hive.

After driving past one more time, Connor parks the car a block or so away. We get out, my stomach doing twisty things. For all we know, we're walking into a trap. Nothing in our limited communication had hinted at our acquaintance with any other vampires, but what if someone recognized our names and has sussed out our link to Trajan?

Connor gives me a confident nod and I square my shoulders. Only one way to find out.

A gender-indefinite person answers our knock, and Connor speaks with authority. "We're here to see the Viscount Baltinglass."

I stand at Connor's side, silently envying the crocheted outfit our greeter is wearing. Their cropped top and low-slung trousers are made of flowered granny squares that hug their slim body. I'm studying the pattern when Connor's elbow brings me back to the present.

"Your name," he says tersely.

"Sorry." I shrug at Granny Squares. "I'm David Collins, and that's a cool"—I wave my hand in their direction—"outfit."

Granny Squares smiles absently. "No need to butter me up. Lord Baltinglass instructed me to let you in."

I give another shrug. Some people can't take compliments. Granny Squares stands aside, pulling the door open wider. I take that as an invitation and beat Connor across the threshold. My ears pop, as if there's been a sudden change in cabin pressure. I glance at Connor, who raises his eyebrows slightly. Must have spells in place to keep out the riffraff. I just hope those spells let us pass if we need to make a quick exit.

We pause and wait for Granny Squares to close the door. They hurry past without even a glance. We follow because we don't have many other options. No effing way I'm going to wander around a vampire's lair without an escort. Besides, if I'm lucky I'll be able to ask Granny Squares where they shop.

They stop in front of a closed door, turning to face us with one hand on the knob. "Lord Baltinglass and the others are downstairs. Be careful. The light is poor." They stand aside, open the door, and wave us through.

Connor goes first. I let him get a couple steps down, then follow. Granny Squares is right. The light is shitty. I reach for a wall to steady myself and behind me, the door slams.

The shitty light goes out. I scramble for the door, but it's locked.

"Hey!"

CHAPTER TWO

Trajan

I text Sheena to tell her I'll meet her at Ralph's. She's done at The Club, so it was a quiet night or she's left the bartender in charge. It could be either, even on a Tuesday night. I'm regularly surprised how often people want to get tied up and whipped in the middle of the week.

Retracing our route to the grocery store on foot gives me the chance to shake off the bad feelings that have been torturing me since I rose this evening. Jacques has been whispering in my ear, moment by moment pointing out ways I could accomplish the task he set for me.

Connor turns his back, and Jacques whispers *Stab him.*

Connor smiles, and Jacques whispers *Cut out his heart.*

Connor slides into my lap, baring his throat to my fangs, and for the first time all night, I'm able to shut Jacques up.

The peace doesn't last, but at least I feed without draining Connor dry.

I dress for the night: a dark suit with a white button-down, top three buttons open, no tie. I find a red pocket square and put on my gold ring. The nugget's about the size of an almond and in my mind, at least, it's a symbol of my independence from Jacques.

I just wish I could claim that independence in his mind, too.

Sheena's driving her black CRV. I climb in the passenger seat and we clasp hands.

"How's it going?" she asks without letting go.

I squeeze her hand. "Rough."

"I'm here if you want to talk about it."

I almost laugh. "Nah. There's nothing to say."

We give each other another squeeze and let go. Sheena's been my best friend for over fifty years. She's an Amazon, the daughter of a priestess. She's also the most popular Domme at my club, and when she's not tying people up, she works as a bodyguard to the stars.

And there's nobody — *nobody* — I'd rather have beside me in a fight.

"I'd like to go by my condo. We've been jumping from place to place, but the condo is pretty much a fortress. I want to kick Levy out and move us in."

She doesn't say anything, just puts the car in gear and backs us out of our parking spot.

"It makes more sense. I'm tired of the constant churn."

"You're not worried that Levy's done something that'll make it possible for Jacques to break through your defenses?"

I snort a laugh, not willing to admit that my maker is in my head *all the damned time*.

"So you want to go up there tonight?"

She's got one hand on the wheel, the other on the cupholder. I rest my hand on hers. "If you don't mind. I can tell Levy to scram and then we can check the defenses."

"Scram." She chuckles. "Sure, grandpa."

I give her a mock punch and she laughs. Between Ralph's and Santa Monica I run through the list of safety features I'd had installed in the condo when I bought the place years ago. Things like motion sensor alarms and auto-locks that respond only to my thumbprint. I'd also had it warded with a three-layer system of spells. Each had an increasingly horrible consequence for breaking it, so that no manner of creature, no matter how powerful, could get through all three alive.

"All of it should still work." I scrape my fingers through the long lock of hair that insists on falling in my face. Maybe I should start cutting it, even though I'd have to do it again every day when I rise. "If we can get rid of Levy, let's bring in a witch and have the wards reset."

She's got both hands on the wheel and taps a rhythm with her thumbs. "Sure, as long as Jacques hasn't brought in a more powerful witch to set some kind of subterranean spell."

"Subterranean spell?"

"Something that could be triggered if you remove the current wards or that isn't detectable by whoever you hire to reset them."

"Have I ever told you you're really good at borrowing trouble?"

She grins and slides us through traffic. "Let's start with Levy and see where that gets us."

Jonathan Levy is the definition of cool. He's slight, wiry even, but his dark eyes and gorgeous cheekbones have such charisma he gives the impression of size. He's also whip smart and hell in an argument. Sheena parks in the lot next to my condominium building and we both get out of the car.

"You could stay here."

Another chuckle. I seem to have a knack for making her laugh tonight.

"As if. For all you know, Jacques Betancourt is waiting for you."

He won't be—I don't think—but I give up the fight. Having Sheena at my side always makes things go better, if for no other reason than I take fewer risks out of concern for her safety.

Besides, Levy likes to talk, and Sheena's an expert at ending a conversation.

I could let myself in the front door, and I will if he doesn't answer the call. He does, though, and I tell him it's me and ask if we can come up. His only response is to hit the button that unlocks the door. Sheena opens it and gives me a fortifying smile.

"How bad can it be?" she murmurs.

I don't answer. The possibilities are endless.

We ride the elevator to the twelfth floor in silence. When I knock on the condo door—*my* condo door—she clears her throat, so I'm glancing at her when the door pops open.

Startled, I turn. Levy stands in the doorway, his dark hair artfully tousled, the heavy silk of his shirt flowing over his body, open at the throat and at the cuffs.

"It's my landlord." His smile shows a hint of fang. I wait to see if he'll invite us in. He doesn't. "Come to see his lowly tenant. I wonder why, after all these months, he'd choose tonight to show up."

"I hope I'm not interrupting." I try to match his disinterested tone.

"I've only just come back from a meeting, and your timing amuses me."

"I'm amusing?"

His smile turns predatory. "You were the meeting's main topic. It seems you've been a very bad boy, and Jacques is most unhappy."

At my side, Sheena tenses. I will myself to stay relaxed. *Never let them see you sweat.* "Maybe it's Jacques who's out of line."

Because that's the crux. I've been loyal to Jacques for a hundred and fifty years, doing anything he asked without question. The command to kill Connor, though. That was too much.

"Careful." Levy leans toward me. "I'd invite you in, but I'm entertaining," he whispers. "If you were smart, you'd leave here. Go as far as you can."

"And have Jacques chase me wherever I go."

His head tilts and his eyes widen as if I've said something stupid. "You can go farther than he can." His lips barely move when he forms the words.

"Tray won't leave because Connor won't," Sheena says. "Not until he finds the Princess."

"Gah." Levy steps away from us. We've outlived his brief moment of good humor.

My humor's gone, too. "I want my condo back. How soon can you be out?"

"Now. Never. My invitation to stay has always been dependent on you." He shows me his palms.

"If you want me to go, I'm gone, although"—he glances over his shoulder—"it honestly might go better for me if you stake me here."

"What?"

Levy's laugh is tinged with hysteria. "Betancourt was quite clear in his desire to see you dead."

"You're supposed to kill me?"

He waves me off, lips twisted in half a smile, and starts to spew a whole bunch of words about all the reasons he hates living in my condo anyway.

"I'll be out by Friday at the latest." With that parting shot, he closes the door before I can say thank you—not that I'd planned on it anyway. There was something weird here, something I couldn't identify. I glance at Sheena and she's staring at the closed door, her brows drawn together.

"Wonder who he's entertaining," she says, and I shrug in response.

"Let's go. I'm less concerned with who he's entertaining than whether he was joking when he said I should stake him."

Sheena gave me an exasperated look. "I didn't hear a joke. You're fifty years older than he is and could kick his ass without trying. I mean, if he didn't talk you to death first."

"True." With another shrug, I head back to the car.

Sheena drives and I ponder. I've had an idea in mind, one I think I'm ready to act on. When we're close to the place David, Connor, and I are staying, I ask Sheena if she'll come in for a minute. David left me a key card and I use it to let us in.

The house is quiet, empty. David and Connor aren't back from their visit with Rollie, which adds to my tension. *Damn.*

"Grab a chair." I wave in the direction of the big dining table. "I need to get something. I'll be right back."

She perches on the church pew, phone out while she waits. I go to the windowless vampire room, looking for the packet I've been carrying around with me since we left Jacques' big house in Beverly Hills. In it is everything I own: deeds, stock certificates, the works. And at the top of the packet is my will.

Or what passes for a will when you're a vampire.

I'm sure it wouldn't be considered a legal document, but it'll stand in our world. In it, I give everything to Connor and David.

Everything except The Club, which I want Sheena to have.

I carry the folder to her. "Here." I hold it out and for a moment she simply stares at me.

"What's this?"

"Hang onto it until we're living someplace stable. If you want to put it in a safe deposit box, I'll pay the fee."

Her eyes narrow as if she's sorting through arguments for and against.

"Just…take it. If something happens to me, Jacques will get everything" — I give a little shrug, palms up — "if he can find it."

Without a word, she sets the packet on the table and stands. Sheena, my truest, indestructible friend, wraps her arms around me and holds me close. "He won't find it," she murmurs against my chest.

We hold each other for a long time, Sheena and I, until the niggling worry about David and Connor starts to gain steam and I let her go.

CHAPTER THREE

T he door's locked." David sounds pissed. I don't blame him.

"For a viscount, this guy's hospitality is lacking." I feel my way down another step. David follows, keeping a hand on my shoulder. "If this is a basement, maybe there's another way out."

I keep heading down. "Except there are no basements in Los Angeles, especially this close to the beach."

David stumbles on a step, putting more pressure on my shoulder.

"So…where are we?"

I reach the bottom, or at least I've run out of steps, and glance at him over my shoulder, testing my theory. "Well, I can't see your aura, and we're in a basement that shouldn't exist. At a guess I'd say we're in some sort of alternate reality."

"Wait. What?" David's voice squeaks just a little. "Like, the Netherworld?"

"No, I don't—"

He shakes my arm. "What's that?"

I scan the area. To our right there's a light patch in the darkness. David scoots around me and heads for it. I follow, wondering where it is we're being led.

It's not an overhead light, more like a portrait on the wall with a spotlight aimed at it. A portrait or a mirror. David and I are both reflected in it until we fade in a spill of milky light and a new figure emerges.

The Elven Princess, Tatiana. She has no discernable aura, which makes me wonder if she's real or a figment of my imagination. Still, her delicate beauty is unmistakable, her hair long and auburn and her golden-brown eyes glowing.

"Where are you?" I ask, or maybe I just think the words. She meets my gaze directly, although when she responds, I don't see her lips move.

"The demon has my body and he's trapped me here in the Netherworld. You *must* find my body before he destroys me."

"I'm trying. I will." I harden my voice to cover the swell of insecurities. *Yes, we'd be a lot better off if I'd found her already. Fuck me.*

"You must."

"The Morrigan—"

She cuts me off with a laugh. "Ananda Pendragon has her gifts, but she's more likely to burn it all down without considering the costs."

And I'm a better choice? "Yeah, I'm trying to cut her out as much as possible. I've been working with Sam Kowalski to bring in some of your people to help."

She nods at that, her lips pursed. "Hmm. Better to have left him out of it. He'll make…trouble."

David doesn't appear to be paying us any attention, so I line up my questions. "Where are you now? Can you tell me anything to help me find your body?"

"I must go," the Princess says. "We're near the ocean, close enough to hear the waves. I can't tell…"

Her image fades before her voice does, and I end up staring at myself in the glass. If what I've seen is true, the Princess thinks of the Morrigan as an ally and Sam Kowalski as a complication. *Damnú.*

David huffs a laugh and I turn to him. "What do you think?"

"About what?" he asks.

"About the Princess?"

"Who?" His brows draw together in confusion. "What are you talking about?"

"The conversation I just had with Princess Tatiana."

"I didn't see the Princess. Wait. You didn't see my pack or whatever?"

"Your pack? Nope. Not at all."

We're staring at each other, perplexed, when the lights come on and there's a round of applause from above us. I spin around, gun drawn.

"Well done. Both of you. Very well done."

A man comes down the stairs, clapping enthusiastically. He's about halfway between me and David in height, but thicker, stocky. He's wearing a white button-down, the weight of the fabric showing its quality, with a burgundy silk cravat at his throat. He should look precious as hell, but from the gold ring on his pinky to his black velvet slippers he looks polished, refined.

"In case you hadn't guessed, I'm your host, Roland FitzEustace, Viscount Baltinglass." He's got an accent, but I can't pin it down to time or place. "And you're acquainted with my dear friend Trajan Gall."

David twitches as if he's fighting a giggle and I incline my head, letting a show of respect hide my smile. "We are."

"Please do come up and join the others. I apologize for the oddness of your welcome. I needed you both to look into the Mirror of Derised."

"Something you borrowed from Hogwarts?" David's tone is just polite enough.

"Exactly." The Viscount gives David another burst of applause. "I had a witch make me a copy so I could see what my guests really want. You two passed."

He turns toward the stairs and we follow. They're marble and when I make the mistake of looking over my shoulder, I see they're dissolving into nothing.

Great. This guy has power to waste. We need to be very, very careful.

We follow him to a large room with white plaster walls and exposed wooden beams. A variety of upholstered furnishings fill the space. I count two couches, a loveseat, and four or five chairs, each from a different time period and covered with a different fabric. Somehow the cacophony of color makes a coherent whole, although I'll have a headache if we stay here too long.

The viscount takes a seat in the center of the largest couch, a blue and orange floral number straight out of 1950. His entourage, made up of half a dozen or so vampires along with the same number of other supernatural creatures, array themselves around the room, leaving David and me standing in the middle of the floor. No one reads human. Their auras add to the kaleidoscope of color, and it feels like we're on display.

I don't like it. The vibe here is jangling my nerves and my gun weighs heavy in my shoulder holster. David's not armed — well, except for his wolf he isn't — but he'll bitch like hell if he ruins his jeans by shifting. I mean, shifting will heal any wounds he suffers, but it won't fix the clothing he shreds when it happens.

The young person who met us at the door takes a seat on the floor at the viscount's feet. They're the picture of androgyny, even more so than David, and I default to plural pronouns until someone tells me otherwise. David's giving them a covetous look, though most likely he's jealous of that crocheted outfit.

"So, you're acquainted with Trajan and you're not here to cause me and mine any trouble." The viscount rests his hand on the androgynous person's head, the way you would a pet. "What are you here for?"

Posing the question of how to break with your vampire maker in front of the viscount's whole crew would be an epically stupid move. "Lord Baltinglass—"

"Call me Rollie. Everyone else does."

His entourage responds with a mix of laughter and murmured approval that does little to reassure me.

"Of course. Rollie, then. We're—"

"Is it possible for a vampire to break up with their maker?" David's clarity cuts through the miasma of bonhomie.

Rollie's expression hardens. "Why would you want to know that?"

"Asking for a friend."

I want to kick David in the balls. This is not the right approach, although I can't really say what I'd do different.

"You two are fucking. Each other, I mean. Am I right?" Rollie's gaze is calculating, as if he's weighing our relative value. "We're always up for a floor show."

David and I share a glance. His expression is somewhere between *Is this for real?* and *No fucking way*. With that question answered, I turn to our host. "Are you saying we can trade a performance for the information we need?"

Rollie's grin turns gleeful. "Maybe. If you need encouragement, Desmond over there is a satyr."

The man he gestures toward looks relatively human, except for the heartbeat when he lets us see his true form, goat legs and hairy cock and all. The woman closest to him leans over and scratches the cleft between his human legs with long black fingernails and he growls in response.

I don't need to look at David to know his answer. "I'm sorry to have bothered you. We'll leave you to your evening."

As a unit we turn. The door is gone, replaced by a smooth, white wall.

"Not yet!" Rollie's laughter makes my teeth grind and his entourage brays and applauds. I spin around, muscles tensed for a fight.

"Don't leave so soon. You're the most entertaining thing we've seen all week." Rollie rises, sauntering toward us. "Such a pretty little wolf" — David growls — "and you." He reaches toward my chest but I move aside so he doesn't touch me. "You're the wild card, aren't you."

I don't respond. I've got my gun loaded with silver bullets, but there are too many of them and too few of us.

Rollie and I lock gazes until I sense him probing in places he shouldn't be, and I shut him out. He turns his attention to David and finally murmurs, "Yes. I think you've got the balls for it."

He gives a sharp clap. "Rio, come with me. The rest of you entertain yourselves while we see our guests out."

The androgenous one, Rio, joins us and we head for a doorway that hadn't been there three minutes ago. Goddamn magicians.

I take the lead with David tight by my side. We're steps from the foyer. Rio slides past, murmuring something to David. Reaching the door, I turn to Rollie, waiting to see what he's going to do next.

"Right, so the short answer is, it's impossible for a vampire to break with his maker." Rollie gives us an expectant look, and it's pretty obvious what he's not saying.

"Then we'll need to destroy the maker." I put it out there just to make sure we're all on the same page.

Rio hums something vaguely affirmative and Rollie shushes them. "Betancourt and I have no love for each other, but still, if anybody asks, you didn't hear it from me."

I'm not sure who would ask. It's not like vampires have some kind of governing body the way wolves do. The Securitas might step in if a couple of vampire sires started a fight, but only if humans were affected. "We'll keep that in mind. Any idea where Jacques might be hiding?"

The look he gives me is pensive. "Gall should know the answer to that. If he hasn't told you yet, there's a reason."

David looks up from inspecting Rio's outfit. "He doesn't know. He'd tell us if he did."

"Ahh, a loyal one." Rollie takes hold of Rio's hand and draws him away. "I've told you all I can. Jacques Betancourt has more enemies than he has friends right now, and it's his own damned fault. It never pays to piss off your strongest ally. Come, Rio. By now Desmond is balls deep in someone. Let's make a bet on who it is."

Rio gives David a shy wave and follows Rollie, Roland FitzEustace, Viscount Baltinglass, whatever the hell his proper name is. David just laughs, shaking his head. "Let's get out of here. I'm afraid the crazy is catching."

We share a smile and head out the door. If killing Jacques Betancourt is the only way to free Trajan, then that's what we'll do.

We just have to find him first.

It's only when we're in the RAV4 that I think to ask David what he'd seen in Rollie's magic mirror.

"Nothing," he says, for once sounding like a sullen teenager.

"No, really. What was it?"

He sits quiet for a while, staring out the window. "It was all of us," he says softly. "You, me, Trajan, and Abby too. My cousin Marcus. Another girl I didn't recognize. All of us in the same place, and all of us pack."

"That sounds pretty great."

"Yeah." He sighs, then shoots me a sly glance. "Maybe someday. In the meantime, do you believe Rollie when he says Tray knows where

Jacques is hiding? Because, man, if we're back to keeping secrets..."

I snort and keep my eyes on the road. We'd sure learned a lesson about keeping secrets, and if Trajan was back at it again, things were going to get rough.

CHAPTER FOUR

We find Trajan sitting in one of the big dining chairs, engrossed in something on his laptop. "What the hell took you so long?" he asks, like maybe we stopped for cocktails on the way.

David laughs at his irritation. "Oh, sugar bear, have we got a story for you."

"Sugar bear?" I raise an eyebrow at David.

He sticks out his tongue, plops himself at the end of the church pew, and points at the laptop. "Whatcha doin'?"

"I've made a map of Jacques' safe houses, showing which of the ones we've checked out and which we haven't. He has to be at one of them."

Steadying myself with a deep breath, I prepare to prove how much I've changed. No secrets, remember? "Are you sure you don't know which one?"

He fixes me with a dark stare. "What?"

The ice in his tone makes it very clear I've fucked up, but damn. On the one hand, I know he would have told us. On the other…

"Let's start at the beginning." David pats the pew, inviting me to sit. "We had an interesting conversation with your good friend Rollie."

"Ha." Trajan closes the laptop. "Is that what he said? I should have warned you. The guy's a compulsive liar."

I sling off my jacket and crowd onto the church pew, which is about as comfortable as I'd imagined it would be. "He does spin a good yarn."

"So tell me what happened."

David runs through the whole story, including a lot more detail than I would have. For example, I wouldn't have mentioned the name of the boutique where Rio bought their fabulous crocheted outfit, but then I was more concerned with who might be armed and which supernatural was most likely to try to kill us.

"And he really said I knew where Jacques is hiding? That bastard." Trajan's eyes are the color of a storm cloud and his skin is paler than normal.

I lean forward on my elbows. "He also said you'd need to kill Jacques to be free of him."

"That doesn't surprise me."

The fatalism in Trajan's voice cuts me deep. "We'll figure something out."

"If he's a chronic liar," David says slowly, "and you're not keeping Jacques' location from us—"

"Of course I'm not." The words fall like shards of glass.

"All right." I raise my hands, showing him my palms. "We believe you, but David's point is good. Trying to pick out the truth from Rollie's stream of bullshit might take more time than we have. The princess said she could hear waves breaking. Does Jacques own a place on the ocean?"

"But was it really the Princess? Maybe the mirror somehow amplified our wishes and played back what we wanted to see."

I nudge David with my elbow, pretty convinced he's the only one of us with any common sense. "You could be right." It seems unlikely that I'd make up something like the breaking waves, but maybe I did. Either way, I hope his vision of all of us with his family will prove to be true. He gives me a smile that might be too bright, but I let it go. We need information more than we need to process emotional stuff right now.

"So you managed to get in and out alive, and you may or may not have learned anything useful." Trajan's got his hands crossed on top of the laptop, his errant hank of hair hanging in his face. There's something defeated about him that I really dislike.

"Did Sheena come by?" I ask, mainly to give us something else to chew on.

He nods. "We went by my condo. Levy's been camped out there the last couple of months, but he says he can be out by Friday."

"Your beautiful condo with the view of forever?" David bounces a little in his seat.

"It's safer than any of these other places we've been staying."

I raise a finger, not sure I should protest. Can't help myself. "Except Jacques knows that place and will be looking for you there."

"It's warded six ways to Sunday."

"Yeah, but..." I look at David for help. We'd talked about this before and decided the condo wasn't safe enough. David's watching Trajan, so he doesn't see my concern.

"Hey, Guido, you know what I think?" David asks. "I think we should go to bed and forget about all the bullshit for a while." He gets up, puts his hands on Trajan's shoulders, and shoves gently. At first Trajan resists, but then he relaxes and allows David to climb into his lap. He's not smiling, exactly, but his expression is lighter.

"And how do you plan to distract me?"

David slides a finger down Trajan's chest. "I'm sure I'll come up with something."

I could get up and work on Trajan from behind, massage his shoulders, play at biting his neck. I don't. Until we get this Jacques thing settled, I don't want to test Trajan's endurance. I'm not afraid he'll kill me — hell, I'm pretty sure he couldn't anyway — but keeping some distance seems kinder, somehow. Besides, watching David grind in Trajan's lap is its own turn-on.

"Bed, puppy. Let's go."

David latches onto Trajan's neck. He growls when Trajan stands, worrying the flesh with his teeth. Trajan smacks his ass and, catching my gaze, nods in the direction of the bedrooms. He leads, and I follow.

And halfway down the hall, David looks up from Trajan's neck and gives me a lewd wink. We've only got a couple of hours until sunrise, not enough time for a meaningful search for Jacques, and this anonymous house in the middle of the 'burbs is about as safe as I can make it.

Might as well have some fun.

Or let them have some fun. While I watch. I've known Trajan Gall a while, and the shadow over his aura is new. Even when we first reconnected, in those wild days when he and David were on the run, he hadn't looked like this. Now all I see is the darkness, his struggle, and I vow to myself that if someone needs to stake Jacques Betancourt, I'll do the honors.

By the time they get to the vampire room, David's got Trajan's shirt open and he's working on the fly of Tray's jeans. The place has minimal decoration, a bed with a plain comforter and a cheap-ass dresser, as if the owner figured a vampire who was going to die all day wouldn't care either way. I lean against the door jam, arms crossed, unable to help my grin.

Because really, watching the two sexiest men I know get it on is no hardship. Eventually I'll have to reach down and take care of myself, but for now I'm happy to be a voyeur.

Trajan's sitting on the bed with David straddling him. There's a pause in the action while David takes his own shirt off, and then he pushes Trajan flat, rising over him on hands and knees.

"Come on, Tony." David sits back and grabs at the waistband of Trajan's jeans. "Lemme see the good stuff."

I sidle further into the room so I have a profile view. David pulls Trajan's cock free of his jeans and wraps both hands around it. Trajan inhales deeply when David starts to stroke him. The young werewolf flashes me a grin, then leans forward so he can catch one of Trajan's nipples in his teeth.

"Hell." The word is more of a gasp, but I get it. My own nipples tingle in response to Trajan's obvious arousal.

They carry on for a while, David stroking and nipping until Trajan's writhing underneath him. Then something happens, like a flip has switched, and Trajan grabs hold of David's wrist.

"Wait. Where's *amoré mio*?" He looks around, eyes still heavy with lust.

"I'm here, *mo shíorghrá*. David is taking good care of you and I'm having a fine time watching."

David shakes free of his grasp. "This is for you, Guido. Shut up and come." He starts stroking wildly while easing back on his heels. I reach for my fly, because my swollen cock is trying to tear through the denim I'm wearing. David adjusts himself so that every down stroke brings Tray's cock to his lips.

And every time his cock hits David's lips, Trajan whimpers.

Dia á sábháil, I'm going to cream my jeans.

David squirms around again, this time pulling his own dick out. What fate didn't give him in stature it made up for in size. He gives himself a couple strong pulls, then goes back to work on Trajan.

Soon Trajan's groaning, David's humping his thigh, and I'm braced against the wall, jerking myself for all I'm worth. They're gorgeous, my men, half-dressed and wholly debauched. My climax hits me before they're through, taking me by surprise and sending me to the floor when my knees will no longer hold me.

So they're at my eye level when David swallows Trajan to the root. The vampire arches off the bed, his cry of pleasure a sound that I'll hold in my soul. Trajan goes limp and David ruts against him, growling his aggressive pleasure, and in short order he starts to buck and curse.

We're done. Sated. David's face is pressed into Trajan's armpit, but he scoots around so one leg barely reaches me. I cup the sole of his foot and his lips curl in a smile. Trajan makes a sound that's suspiciously like a snore.

It's not quite sunrise when I manage to stand, but Trajan's still out so David and I clean him up and arrange him in his bed. We take the windowed bedroom where the bed wishes it were king-sized, although I for one plan to sleep only for a couple hours.

We've got a vampire sire to find.

I wake to the sound of my phone beeping wildly, punctuated by cursing. "What the hell?"

David's got his laptop open and my phone's on the nightstand, buzzing about every thirty seconds.

"Fucking fuck." He glares at me and points at his computer screen. "The fucking Los Angeles

Were Authority has had a complaint against me and wants to hold a hearing."

"Damn. What's that about?"

"They say I've created an unauthorized pack."

I blink at him, too sleepy to really follow what he's saying. "I mean, your dad knows about…us, right?" David's father, the American Were Authority Alpha. The biggest of the big dogs.

"Of course he knows."

"So who would do something like that?"

"I don't know yet, but I'm going to find out."

"Is there a name on the complaint?"

He snorts a laugh, fingers dancing over the keys. "Nope, but Abby'll know who I can ask. Some dumb fucker is going down."

Glad that I've managed to stay on David's good side, I decide my eyes are focused enough to deal with whoever's texting me.

It's Detective Boudreau from the LAPD, letting me know the supernatural liaison position is open.

I tell him I'll think about it, although I don't think I'll have time to work for the LAPD until we get this thing with Jacques sorted out.

CHAPTER FIVE

Trajan

I rise alone.

As usual, my lovers left me at sunrise and now silence holds my windowless room in thrall. If either of them are in the house, I would know. Music would play, or the ping and rattle of a computer game would prickle my consciousness like nettles.

I could stay here in the darkness. David and Connor are gone, either to find us another place to hide out or to otherwise rescue me from the mess I've made.

Am I jealous that the two of them have found common ground? I barely pose the question before my conscious mind shouts it down. It's only natural that the three of us would have different interests, that there might be things I share with Connor that are different than those I share with David. We're new at this. We need time to get to know each other better.

Time and safety.

I'm about to crawl out of bed when someone knocks on the door. My entire body flinches, more startled than I should be. I try to sit up, to sling my legs over the side of the bed, but I can't move. I lie frozen and the door opens.

Jacques Betancourt walks in, visible even in the darkness.

He flips the switch for the light and takes a seat in the room's lone chair. He looks healthy, vibrant even, and for a moment I just stare. Vampires don't change from day to day, but this is the Jacques I knew a hundred years ago. The last few times I'd seen him, he'd been frailer, gaunt even.

The figure before me sits preening under my appraisal. I want to ask what he wants, but my mouth is as paralyzed as the rest of my body. He's wearing velvet trousers and a silk shirt that's open at his throat. He crosses one leg over the other, hands clasped around his knee. "You didn't know I could do this, did you? You're my child, and I can visit you whenever I want."

There's a smugness to his tone that makes me want to snap a response. I can't.

He heaves an exaggerated sigh. "Your visit with Levy went well enough. He tells me you want to move back into your condo."

Fear for the trouble I may have caused Levy joins the roil of anger and frustration in my belly. I can't even blink.

"See, Levy understands me. I asked all my scions to notify me if my prodigal son contacted them, and he did." Jacques leans forward, bracing himself with his palms on his knees. "But you, my prodigal one, have not done the one thing I've asked."

His eyes turn hard, boring into mine. "Do you remember when we first met?" He speaks barely louder than a whisper. "Where were you going to sleep, the night I met you?"

It's a good thing I can't respond because who knows what I'll say. We met one stifling August night in 1850, in some nameless town along the Mississippi where I'd been trying to win enough at cards to afford a room with an actual bed, instead of bunking in some dark stable.

"You were a strapping big boy, weren't you? You caught my eye the moment I walked into the saloon. I'd never made another into such as us before I met you. You were my first, my oldest companion. My pride."

He's trying to sound wistful, but I'm not fooled. This is a demonstration of power, a reminder of how thoroughly he owns me.

"I saw something in you that night. Your determination." He tilted his head. "Or was it desperation? You barely owned the clothes on your back, let along something clean to change into."

A knee-jerk flood of shame drowns out all other emotions. Shame I learned at Jacques' knee. My memories of those days contained as much determination as desperation. If I only had one change of clothes, at least I was alive to wear them.

"Why could you not do as I asked? I'm about to take a step that will leave me stronger than ever, but instead of having you join me, I'll be forced to destroy you, too, along with that Danaan spawn."

He shrugs, as if talking about my final death doesn't trouble him. "I might keep the wolf, though. He could be useful."

Though I can't speak, he must see the rage in my eyes. Rage and helplessness. My muscles are locked in a fight to move.

Standing, Jacques brushes smooth his velvet trousers and fixes me with another sorrowful look. "Consider yourself warned, Trajan Gall. I intend to send you to your final death, along with your friend MacPherson."

With that, he leaves the room. I blink and find I can move. The light is still on, but there's no chair. The room's so small there's barely enough space to walk around the foot of the bed.

I draw in great shuddering breaths. My maker had paid me a visit, at least spiritually. I stagger out of bed, hoping Connor and David will return soon. They need to know what Jacques is planning.

I need to warn them, and then we need to come up with a strong defense. Lord Rollie Blowhard might have been lying, but he wasn't wrong.

I'll only be free of Jacques when I send him to his final death.

Opening the door of the vampire room, I'm surprised to hear music, the kind made by Tibetan singing bowls. David is in the middle of the living room, balanced on his head, elbows braced at right angles providing stability. Connor sits nearby, staring over the top of his laptop. The sun has nearly set, the blue light from Connor's laptop mixing with the warm glow from the overhead fixture.

"I thought you were gone." The words escape before I can stop them. Connor's expression lightens and David slowly lowers his lean legs to the ground, one at a time.

"Some detective from the LAPD is after me to apply for the supernatural liaison position." Connor smiles ruefully. "I told him I'd think about it, but he keeps texting."

"Because you had so much fun last time," David grumbles. He's sitting with his back straight, his knees wide, and his feet pressed together. "And I spent the afternoon planning someone's demise."

"Whose?" I can't help but chuckle, because he's plainly exaggerating. At the same time, his statement is uncomfortably close to my own agenda for the evening.

"Whoever reported me to the goddamn Los Angeles County Were Authority." He stretches forward until his nose touches the ground, his languid motion at odds with the snap in his tone.

Connor picks up the explanation. "Someone filed a complaint saying he's formed an unauthorized pack."

I glance from Connor to the knot of bleached hair on the top of David's head, and for a moment, I don't want to disrupt their ordinary concerns with my drama.

On the other hand, I can't demand their honesty if I'm going to keep secrets and anyway, the fact that we're in some short-term rental instead of someplace more permanent means they're part of my drama anyway.

"Jacques made a visit."

"What?" Connor radiates concern while David straightens fast enough to hurt.

"He knows we're here?"

"I'm not sure. He wasn't physically present. I believe his spirit came into the vampire room, although he could have keyed off my essence somehow without having an actual address."

"Still." David's already on his feet. "That tells me it's time to move along."

Connor's nodding like he agrees. "What'd he say?"

I tell them the threats he made, leaving out his digs at my past. I have almost one hundred fifty years of distance between myself and the young man who'd done what he needed to survive. The past is finished.

"We can't destroy Jacques until we find him," Connor says, closing his laptop. "And I agree with David. This place isn't safe. We need to leave now."

We're interrupted by a heavy hand knocking hard on the front door. We both freeze for a heartbeat, and then Connor tips his head in the direction of the vampire room.

"Go, and I'll see who it is."

I want to argue but whoever it is knocks again. I don't leave, but I don't follow Connor to the door, either. He opens it to find two men out front. They introduce themselves as LAPD detectives, and they want to talk to us about a fire in a condominium on the twelfth floor of a complex in Santa Monica.

My condo, now apparently gutted by fire.

The one in the grey suit is Franklin and the one in the brown-and-beige number is Gonzales. Franklin says the fire started in the early morning hours.

"When's the last time you were in the condo?" Gonzales has the bored tone of someone who has seen it all and can barely be bothered.

It would be easy enough to send them out the door with the *suggestion* that they haven't learned anything useful, but I want to know if they've found Levy. "Last evening. I went to tell the person who was living there that I wanted him out."

Franklin whips a small notebook out of his pocket. "And who was that?"

"A vampire named Jonathan Levy."

Most ordinary people know that supernatural beings exist, and surely police detectives have crossed paths with the unknown before, but they both look like I've punched them in the gut. I give them a minute and then keep talking. "I take it you didn't find any bodies."

They share a glance before Gonzales speaks. "No. No bodies."

Which means either Levy got out or one of the piles of ash belonged to him.

Damn it.

"Is there a reason you had a vampire living in your condo?" Gonzales asks. Franklin's face is the same color grey as his suit.

I just smile, showing fang. Connor must sense that I'm out of fucks because he slides between me and the two detectives. He introduces himself, handing them both his cards.

"I'm a little confused why a couple of police detectives would be talking to us about a fire."

Gonzales grins. "Maybe because the fire investigator had questions about how the fire was started."

Franklin has none of his partner's bravado. He's staring at Connor's card, recognition dawning so brightly I can see it. "You and Adam Smith…" His voice trails to nothing, but it's enough to make Gonzales give Connor's card a closer look.

Maybe I am out of fucks. "Thank you for the visit, gentlemen. If you managed to track us here, you'll also be able to see that I bought that condominium the year it was built. If I was going to torch the place, what possible reason could I have for doing it now?"

"I'm not sure. Why don't you tell us?" Gonzales is still talking big, but his bravado is showing cracks.

Connor puts a quelling hand on my arm. "So answer me this. How did you track Trajan to this house?"

A soft whimper escapes from Franklin.

"Dispatch," Gonzales says, his affect so flat I can't tell if he's lying. "We got a call from dispatch telling us to come by here and talk to a man about a fire."

"Well." Connor lets the word ring. He crosses his arms, chin lifted. "If you want to talk any more, you're going to have to come up with something better than that."

Connor slides a glance my way and I step forward. "Thank you both. You've been very helpful." Underneath the words, I tell them to get the hell out of here. Now.

They do.

The door closes behind them and Connor and I stand side by side.

"You think Jacques set the fire?" he asks.

"Yup."

"And gave this address to dispatch."

I'm damn near groaning with frustration. "Yes."

David pops out of the bedroom. "Are the Men's Wearhouse refugees gone?"

Connor's the only one with the energy to laugh. My jaw's clenched so tight I might crack a tooth. He slides his hand down my arm, interlacing our fingers. "I'm sorry about your place."

"Me too." *And if I've done something that sent Levy to his final death…*

"Okay, here's the deal," David says. "I've booked us a hotel room but since someone on Jacques' team twigged my credit card I figure they're likely to look for Connor's too. Instead I used Abby's. I'll Venmo her the cash and we'll be that much harder to find."

Part of me is still furious at the turn of events, yet I reach out for David's hand. Looking from one of my men to the other, I say the only thing I can.

"Thank you."

David's hand is warmer, but it's Connor's grasp that I'm most aware of. His touch and the sound of Jacques Betancourt murmuring in my ear.

Kill him. Kill him. Kill…

CHAPTER SIX

"Was that weird?" David stares at the door Trajan has just walked through. "Yeah, that was weird."

Since David answered his own question, I didn't feel the need to respond. My phone chirped, letting me know I'd received an email.

From Trajan.

The list of all of Jacques' safe houses by neighborhood and street address.

I scan it, buying time because I'm not sure how David's going to respond to what I've got to say.

"We need to pack. Now."

David's command redirects my thinking. Yeah, we need to move on before we do anything else. "I'm on it." We try not to unpack much so that we can leave on a dime if we need to.

He bops off to the bedroom and when he comes back, he's thrown a rainbow striped hoodie over his yoga pants and he's carrying his laptop. "My stuff's in my bag."

I'm not convinced he's telling me the truth — or rather, he might believe all his stuff is in his bag but I'm pretty sure I'll find debris scattered between the bedroom and the bath. I knock on Trajan's door. "I'm going to start loading the car. Let me know when you're ready to go."

He doesn't respond and I don't push it. I gather my toiletries — plus a bottle of shampoo that's pricey enough to piss David off if he leaves it here — and make a stack of our luggage. I take a moment to send off a text and then head for the garage.

Someone's sitting in the passenger seat of the RAV4.

I pause in the doorway, debating whether I should go back and get my gun. The figure's aura is a kind of opalescent silver. Not human, but not run-of-the-mill supernatural either. Closing the door with a bang, I stride toward the vehicle.

The figure watches me, eyes dark, hair a salt-and-pepper cloud around their face. I hit the fob to unlock the driver's side door and get in.

Ananda Pendragon, the Morrigan, gives me an angelic smile.

I nod as a sign of respect for her status as a living god, but don't return her smile. She's trouble, and I'd prefer her normal expression of anger to this.

"You know where she is, don't you." It's not a question, so I don't answer.

"Come, *meascach*. Let's put our differences aside. It's nearly the solstice." Her smile all but compels me to agree.

Still, I resist. She looks older than when I'd seen her last, her hair grey, her skin weathered. She is the triune goddess, and though she can take any form she wishes, she's chosen to appear as the crone.

And I don't trust her in any form.

"*Onóir amháin*, I cannot help you find the person you seek." I almost point her at Jacques, but that would give the Morrigan an advantage. I need to get to the Princess first, along with her elven brethren.

The next instant confirms my decision. The kindly crone disappears, replaced by the Morrigan, the living god. Her anger fills the vehicle, making it hard to breathe.

"You *will* find the Princess Tatiana or your lovers will suffer."

For a moment I wonder how she'd deal with a bodach. Instead, I laugh. "Is that all you got, Grandmother? You alternate between demands and threats and I'm supposed to, what? Be grateful my Tuatha Dé Danaan relatives have taken notice of my presence, that I can shift into a horse whenever I want to?" *Because damn.* "I've been an outcast since the day I was born. Your displeasure doesn't mean a whole lot to me."

Somewhere my mother is sobbing into her cereal. She raised me to have the utmost respect for all members of the Tuatha Dé, and here I am, mouthing off to one of the oldest and strongest.

Seems like embodying the specter of death had more of an effect on me than I thought.

While I'm musing, the Morrigan draws power to herself, until her aura is a blinding white light. I sit back with my arms crossed, squinting at her. She grows so bright I have to shut my eyes and then she goes brighter still.

And when I'm starting to think her game plan is to fry my brain with her evil light, she disappears.

Well, not completely.

"You'll start a war, *meascach.* Your lover is a vampire and you're siding with the elves. That can only end in disaster."

With that, she really is gone. I open my eyes to find David in the doorway, staring at me.

I roll down the car window. "Just a little family business."

He gives a full body shudder. "When a member is in danger, the rest of the pack can sense it."

"I wasn't in danger, not really."

He tilts his head, fists planted on his hips. "Don't even go there, Pookie. Whatever that was grew hair on my chest, and I won't have it."

I climb out, relieved that my knees don't give way. Because David's not wrong. I can pretend I wasn't in danger all day long, but in truth I was ready to play my ace if I had to.

And the specter of death shouldn't be anybody's ace in the hole.

I don't really have time to worry about the consequences of pissing off a living god, because we need to move along. David's booked us a two-room suite in a hotel off Sunset, the kind of place where the bathrooms are *toilettes* and the coffee stand is *la grande buffet*.

Which is to say the "two-room suite" is a decent-sized bedroom with a closet large enough to fit a twin mattress. As soon as he walks in, David's lips twist as if he smells something awful.

"Be careful," I say. "Your face'll freeze that way."

"This place has delusions of adequacy." He plops onto the bed, hands in his lap as if they might get dirty. Trajan is a silent presence and I'm desperate to find a way to help him.

Since I can't disagree with David, I get the last bag out of the RAV4, planning my approach. I've had a response to the text I sent earlier: Colonel Poole from the Elites is willing to meet me.

I have no intention of going back into the service, but we could sure use their resources.

Trajan, his hair slicked back and his expression blank, excuses himself shortly after we arrive, shutting the door on his glorified closet. His suffering makes me sick, and the only way to fix things is to find where Jacques is hiding.

Find him and destroy him.

"Do you think we should try and track down that other vampire sire, Delia Packard?" David's hands pause on the keyboard, his expression still stuck in the stinky sneer.

"I have an errand I want to run first, and…" I rake the hair out of my face so I can meet his gaze head-on. "I think one of us should stay here. I don't think we should leave him alone."

David's expression is one of wisdom. "Sure. You go do your thing, and when you get back, I'll run out for a few."

"That's fair."

He sets his laptop aside and comes over to me, taking my hands in his. "When we get through this, I think we should make date night a regular thing."

"Absolutely, *mo mhuirnin*." I can't help but smile at his optimism. "We can have date nights, and dress up and act slutty nights, and stay home and cuddle nights, and any other thing you can think of."

He rises on his toes and kisses me, a soft, sweet gesture that does more to reassure me than anything else.

"I'll be back in an hour or so," I say. In the interest of transparency, I could tell him I'm going to meet with Poole, but I decide I'd rather report good news than to get his hopes up for nothing.

And then I change my mind and tell him.

He grins despite the smelly hotel room. "If he tries to get you to agree to something in return for his help, don't. You're done with the Elites."

I cup his face and kiss him again. "It's a deal."

Poole wants to meet at Headquarters, on the ninth floor of a building in downtown LA near the Staples Center. Despite the late-night traffic, it doesn't take me long enough to get there to decide how I want to approach things when I see him. I park in the garage underneath the building, and although the security guard stops me, it's only long enough for him to check my ID.

As usual, the elevator is a kaleidoscope of color, the vestiges of every aura that has traveled through the space. The lights in the landing and down the hall are turned low since it's a little after midnight, but fluorescent light streams out of every open door.

I find Poole in the conference room, sitting with his back to the door. He holds himself military straight, his flattop haircut measuring the regulation length. The window across from him shows his reflection, though, and he's got his eyes shut. I hesitate, worried that he's asleep.

"Come in," he says, without opening his eyes.

I come around the table and sit facing him with my back to the window. "Thank you for seeing me on such short notice, sir."

He waves away my thanks. "I figure you wouldn't be here if things were going well."

He'd done a lot to help us get through the debacle with Adam Smith, and while I hadn't gone into any great detail at the time, I'd hinted there were still problems we needed to solve.

"Funny thing. My great-whatever grandmother stopped by this evening."

He rolls his eyes. "She still after the Princess?"

"Guessed it in one. I know where the Princess is, too, more or less."

"Which is it? More or less?"

I decide my best approach is to lay things out for him, then let him tell me where he can help. I tell him about seeing the Princess and about the command Betancourt laid on Trajan, and I sum it up simply. "I want to find Betancourt and send him to his final death."

He looks at me steadily from over his steepled fingers. "I can't spare a team, if that's what you're looking for."

"No, sir. I'm wondering, though, if I could log into the system here. You've got access to data that civilians don't and I'm hoping I can find a way to track Betancourt."

"That's possible, yeah. I can reinstate your account for the next few weeks."

"Thank you, sir."

"Like I said, I can't spare a team, but if you need extra hands, Brodie's in town. As far as I can tell he's making trouble for himself, so it'll do him good to have a project."

I try not to let my ambivalence show. "Thank you, sir. That's very generous of you."

"We could also…" He pauses, scratching at the late-day shadow on his chin. "Melinda Barwell's in town, too. She's a Sensitive, and what our computer can't find she might be able to."

I exhale, beyond pleased. Working with a Sensitive will almost make up for having to keep Brodie occupied. "Yes, sir. I didn't want to ask, but I do think Melinda might be able to help."

"Good. I'll set things in motion and you should be good to go tomorrow." He rises and I follow his cue. Reaching across the table, we shake hands.

"I hope you'll remember this next time I've got a project I think you could help with," he says.

I force my smile to stay in place. "Thank you, sir. I will."

Behind my back, I cross my fingers.

CHAPTER SEVEN

DAVID

Ron's Books and Trinkets on Ventura Boulevard stays open till eleven p.m. I'd only been there once before, riding shotgun for Connor. That time, we'd wanted information about a murderer.

This time, I'm after the witch who works here, because the thing I want isn't likely to be sitting on the shelves.

While I Uber over from our hotel *suite* — and I use that term grudgingly — I divide the ride into worrying about what Connor really promised Poole and wondering if the witch will be working.

Uber dumps me off in a strip mall that's identical to several thousand others in the city of LA. The shop is open, and just like last time, there are more books than I can get my mind around, along with comics and tee shirts and all manner of vintage junk.

Either I'm real lucky or the dude never leaves. Under the earthy vanilla smell of old books, I pick up the scent of his magic, a mix of lavender, sage, and something danker, like the scrapings from the bottom of a trash can. I don't mean that in a bad way. Magic is basically the transmutation of one thing into another, and decay is an essential part of that process and blah blah blah.

At least that's what my high school boyfriend used to claim. He also used to tell me werewolves couldn't catch HIV so it was okay for us to go bareback.

Both of those things might be true, but I didn't want to learn the hard way that he was wrong.

The woman behind the register is goth af, but her magic smells too flowery to be what I'm looking for. I slide between the shelves, dodging random piles of books, stalking the witch. I find him leaning in a doorway in the back, almost as if he's expecting me.

He's Black, his Sly and Robbie tee shirt looks vintage, and his hair is sprinkled with grey. "Whatever you're looking for, we don't have it."

Yeah, he was kind of an asshole the last time I was here, too. "Are you psychic?"

"Nah, but I had Chinese for lunch and my fortune cookie said to watch out for gender-bending werewolves who don't use the common sense god gave them."

That made me laugh. "Gender what? How old are you?"

"Your nails are too clean. Makes me think you don't know how to work."

I hold my clean nails up for inspection. *Nailed it in one.* "I really could use a job." And I'll get one, as soon as we get the Trajan situation settled. It's hard to set up interviews when you're changing location every twenty-four to forty-eight hours. "But more than that, I need a portable ward."

He fakes a belly laugh, slapping the wall. "You want a what, now? Must have to keep the kitties outa your bush, eh?"

"Oh please." I shake my head, fighting a smile. "I've got as much dick as I can handle, but my boyfriend's being harassed, and I need something to keep his…ex outta our hair."

"That big pause before you said ex makes me think there's more going on."

Now this is the tricky part. I want this dude to work with me, but he doesn't need to know the whole story. The fewer people who know Trajan wants to break with Jacques, the safer it'll be for all of us. Right now, it feels like Jacques is playing with us, tormenting Trajan from afar. If it gets back to him that we're actively seeking to sever their bond, I doubt he'd be so restrained.

Especially since the only way to sever their bond is to destroy one of them, and I like Trajan too much to hurt him.

My magician friend waits for me to think all this through, his expression growing more serious.

"What are your rules?" I ask finally.

"Meaning what? I don't eat between seven in the evening and seven in the morning. It's how I keep my girlish figure." He rubs the old tee where it's stretched across his belly.

He's still fucking with me and that's okay. I've got a few more cards to play. "I don't want to ask you to do something that'll cross a line, and I don't want to cause you any trouble. I want a ward that'll keep the bad juju out but that I can pick up and move when I need to."

He crosses his arms over his chest. "Yeah, you said that before, and then you said something about your boyfriend's big pause ex, and before I go making a spell like that, I want to know what I'm getting into. I work as clean as I can, but it's still possible to pick up my…fingerprints, for lack of a better word, from the spell, if Big Pause Ex is so inclined."

Good that he's taking my request seriously. Bad that I hadn't considered that angle. "Okay, so tell me this. What manner of creature is off limits for you?"

He gives an impatient snort. "Quit dodging. What are you up against? If you can't be honest, I can't help you."

I drop my grin. "Vampire."

"Big Pause Ex is a vampire?"

"Yes."

"And your boyfriend is human?"

"No, and I promise you don't want to know the details."

"You got that right." He scratches the back of his head, and I can't tell if he's still with me or if he's about to tell me to take a powder. I give him time to think, and the smell of his magic grows stronger.

"See, I got my little shop, here, and I do spells on the side." He's looking at the floor so I can't get a read on his expression. "And, you know, a place like Ventura Boulevard, we get just about every magical critter you can imagine coming through here.

"All but one. We don't get vampires in here, and you know why?" He meets my gaze dead on.

"Nope."

"I hate them undead fuckers worse than any other thing, living or dead. I don't even know why I'm telling you this..." His voice trails off and I'm torn between prompting him and apologizing for taking him to such a dark place.

"So no, I ain't going to help you mess with a vampire. It's outside my line of work."

Shit. "You know anyone else who might not have your issues? I'm kinda new in town."

His gaze narrows. "I know three or four people who'll charge you for the service, but I can't guarantee any of their spells will work."

A customer comes in, making the little bell over the door jingle. That reminds me. "If you can keep vampires out of here, you must be able to work a spell that'll keep them away from wherever we're staying."

There's a helping of sarcasm in his chuckle. "Oh yeah, I can do it all right. I just don't want whatever you're selling."

His mouth is saying no but his eyes are asking what it's worth to me. Welp, he's the one who brought up money. "If a vampire wasn't involved, how much would you charge for a portable ward?"

"A thousand dollars."

I know damned well he's picked a number out of his ass. "I'll give you fifteen hundred."

Something shifts in his face. "You're cute, you know. You got that pretty twink thing going on with your painted-on jeans and your eyeliner and all, and you make me want to help you." He's gone back to looking at the floor. "But" — he looks up sharply — "I'm not for sale."

He may be talking tough, but there's a flicker of something like interest in his eyes. "All right, if you say so." I take a pointed look around. "You could buy a lot of" — I nudge a stack of books with my toe — "merchandise with fifteen hundred dollars."

"Nope."

He's lost some of his conviction. "What if I throw in a werewolf bodyguard for one night?"

"Now what the hell do I need a bodyguard for?"

"You tell me. You don't spend all your time surrounded by tchotchkes."

He doesn't answer right away, although his only tell is the tension around his eyes. He's interested, all right. Now I just need one more thing to tip him over the edge. "Wanna see something?"

"What?"

I poke my wolf. Hard. We used to do this kind of shit on the daily. "I'm not blowing smoke about the werewolf bodyguard. You'll be protected by one of the best."

"Who is it then? You can't be talking about your own pretty ass."

I point at him and reach for my wolf. The change is slower than it used to be and more painful than I remember, but instead of my human finger with its chartreuse painted nail, I've got a wolf's claw.

And no, the chartreuse didn't transfer to my wolf.

He's too cool to act overtly impressed but his eyes are open wider than they were a minute ago. "What's your name?" There's a new gruffness to his voice.

I extend my human hand. "David Collins."

We shake, but he's blowing a low whistle. "You're *that* dude? Damn."

It's an act of will not to roll my eyes. "Tell me your name so I can start some gossip."

"Albion Bird."

"Albion. I'll remember that."

"And I will remember you, David Collins." He leans against the door frame. "Come by here this time tomorrow and I'll have the ward ready. Oh, and bring cash. I don't take plastic."

"Twelve hundred and a business card with my phone number so you can reach me when you need my service."

"You said fifteen hundred."

"And you said no."

"Fuck you."

"Get in line."

He's glaring, but I know I've won.

"How do you feel about necromancers?" he asks.

Aw shit, Trajan's going to lose his mind. "My boyfriend's not fond of them, but I said I'd do the job and I will."

He's gripping his last reservation with both hands, but then he sighs. "All right. Shit's been slow around here. I'll see you tomorrow afternoon."

I give him a real smile. "Thanks."

And then I text my sister Abby.

Mom needs to transfer $1000 into my account please and don't ask why.

I'll explain when I can. I'm not part of the Collins pack anymore, but I'm still a Collins and Mom's making sure I don't starve to death. Well, Mom and Connor and Trajan. Everyone's been really cool about helping me get back on my feet. I may never be able to pay them all back, but I promise to pay it forward.

Abby responds with a series of emojis that I'm pretty sure translate as "Done and the story better be good."

Thank you.

I Uber back to the hotel and let myself into our *two-room suite*. Connor's at the desk and Trajan's not around.

"Everything okay?"

Connor shrugs and points to his laptop. "I'm comparing the list of Jacques' houses that Trajan sent me with real estate records and deeds recorded by the city."

"Cool," I say, but I'm really looking around the room for any trace of Trajan. Nodding at the door to the vampire room, I ask, "Has he been out?"

Connor's lips grow thin. "No."

Giving him a sympathetic smile, I tap on the door. No answer. I knock louder and hear a muffled…something. Taking the grunt for an invitation, I open the door.

Trajan's lying on the bed. He doesn't move when I open the door, and when I whisper his name he says something like, "Go away."

Now, there's human-still, and vampire-still, and then there's Trajan's utter lack of movement. His "Go away" might as well have been an invitation, because I can't help myself. I cross the small room in two strides and kneel by the bed.

Wolves aren't psychic by nature, but I'd meant it when I told Connor that if a pack member is hurting, I'll know about it.

And Trajan is in agony.

He's radiating pain and his body is rigid, as if he's fighting with every individual muscle to keep from doing…something. I put a hand on his shoulder and the pain crawls up my arm, locking my own muscles in the battle.

"Tray," I whisper. "Oh my god, Tray."

We stay there for a long while and slowly, as if he's unloading some of his burden on me, he relaxes. Connor pokes his head in the door, but I wave him off. He gets it and after a while I hear the door to the suite open and close. Maybe he's gone for food. I've completely lost track of time.

When my knees complain loudly enough, I hitch around and sit on the edge of his bed. He makes a sound, sort of a choked-off sigh and I move closer to him. By the time I hear Connor come back in, Trajan and I are lying side by side and I've got an arm around him, my cheek on his shoulder.

Connor taps on the door and asks if I want anything to eat. "No, I'm good."

He fades away and Trajan draws in a deep breath. "Thank you, David. You shut him up."

"Connor?"

"Jacques. He's in my head, talking and talking and talking."

That sounds appalling. "I didn't know vampires could do that."

He laughs, short and bitter. "I didn't either, but apparently a sire's power expands so they can torment their offspring in situations like this."

"That's fucked up."

"Once the sun rises, I should be okay. He can't get at me when I'm dead, so you can sleep in the other room if you want."

"Nah." I scoot closer. "I'm staying right here."

And I do. After a while, Trajan relaxes completely. I squirm around to get my phone out of my pocket. Sure enough. Sun's up. I set my alarm for two p.m. I might show up at Ron's Books and Trinkets a little early, but my new BFF Albion Bird better have my trinket ready to go.

When Trajan rises, I want to have a ward in place to block that bastard Jacques from getting into his head.

CHAPTER EIGHT

Trajan

The first thing I notice is the quiet. I lie still for several luxurious minutes, reveling in the peace. David's got some jangly disco stuff playing through his laptop and Connor asks him to turn it down, uncharacteristically grumpy. David's laughing answer makes me smile.

Because for the first time in days, there's no one whispering in my ear, demanding that I do anything at all.

The next time Connor bitches about the music, I get up, feeling lighter than I have in a week, maybe two.

I pause in the doorway. I need to clean up some and maybe run a rake through my hair, but there's only one bathroom and neither of my men has noticed me yet. Both of them are on their laptops—David on the bed and Connor at the desk.

Connor's jeans are perfect, his hair is pulled back into the world's smallest ponytail, and the sleeves of his worn UCLA sweatshirt are pushed up to show off his muscular forearms.

David's dressed in his usual kooky grab-bag: a torn white tee shirt stitched together at the shoulders with rainbow-colored yarn, baggy silver trousers, and a slouchy black cap covering most of his bleached hair.

I want them both.

Neither looks up until I clear my throat.

"Hey, it's a vampire sighting." David uncurls from around his laptop and hops off the bed. "You're with us again."

He doesn't stop moving until we're belly to belly. Up close I can see the shadows under his eyes, and I flash on the memory of his body next to mine at sunrise. "I am. Did I miss anything today?"

Connor's nearby, his arms crossed as if he's scared to reach for me. I don't blame him. It can't be pleasant to have someone around who's constantly threatening to kill you.

"David made a deal," Connor says.

I wrap my arms around the werewolf and ask, "What kind and how much did it cost you?"

His smile is brilliant. "I got us a ward that'll block Jacques from messing with you, and whatever it cost is more than worth it."

I'm at a loss. "Oh, puppy…seriously?"

He reaches up and I think he's going to caress me but instead he slaps my face. Gently. "It looks like a hacky sack, to be honest, but we can take it with us when we move from place to place, and it'll keep Jacques out of your head."

I honestly don't know what to say. My lips move, but no sound comes out. Thank you seems like the lamest thing ever, but finally I manage to whisper the words.

"Come on. It's not like Connor has been sitting around bored. He's been trying to figure out which of Jacques' houses is close to the beach."

"Oh?"

David pivots so my arm is around his shoulder and we both look at Connor. His eyes are as tired as David's, and my luck in having them at my side gets me choked up.

"Yeah." Connor's more relaxed, his arms at his side, and for a moment he smiles. "Have you ever heard of Clapton Industries?"

"Doesn't sound remotely familiar."

"Huh. Well, here's what I've got so far." He crosses to the desk and brings up a spreadsheet on the laptop, holding it so we both can see the screen. "The left-hand column is the list of Jacques' houses you sent me, and the middle column are the hits with his name that I get from the city's property records. There's some overlap—those are the green highlights—but as you can see, each list has a couple that aren't on the other."

"He must have houses I don't know about."

"I figured. Some of them are in his own name, and some are in the name of Betancourt LLC, which makes sense."

I nod, waiting to see where he's going with this.

"So here's the weird thing. The entries I've highlighted yellow are also listed under Clapton Industries, with a subtitle like Jacques Betancourt, CEO or thereabouts."

I scan the spreadsheet again. There's one yellow highlight in the list I sent him and another three or four in his second column. "What's the third column?"

"Property listings for Clapton Industries alone, with no mention of Jacques anywhere I could find."

"Really? I've known Jacques for almost a hundred and fifty years. Seems like we'd talk about him starting a new business." I blink, trying to puzzle out the implications of what he's saying. David takes the opportunity to steer me toward the bed, and we sit side by side.

Connor sits in the desk chair. "The really weird thing, though, is that I've seen the name Clapton Industries before."

"Where?" Something in his expression makes me reluctant to hear his answer.

He sets the laptop aside. "Remember when we were in D.C., looking for David in those warehouses?"

David flinches and I pull him closer to me.

"Right before the troll sat on my knee, I was in an office. The desk was covered with invoices and packing slips, and I took a picture of one, so I'd remember the name and address of the business, Frank's Magic Warehouse."

"And?" David asks, always the impatient one.

"The invoice was from Clapton Industries."

A coincidence on that level gives me chills. "Seriously?"

"I wonder if Dad knows anything about either of those businesses." David's sitting straighter than I like, but I stifle the urge to pull him closer. That was easily the worst day of his life. He probably needs the space.

"We did see some pretty suspicious stuff going on." Connor's quick nod says he agrees with me but also that he doesn't want to dig into it any further.

"So, old-timer"—David's laugh sounds forced—"did you google Clapton Industries and see if the name of their CEO is listed on their website?"

Connor sets the laptop back on the desk, giving David a pained expression. "Yeah, you smartass, and there's no mention of Jacques."

"So we have a mysterious business that may or may not be run by Jacques and that may or may not have some kind of tie—however loose—to the American Were Authority in D.C."

Connor nods his head yes, lips pressed together grimly. "Or at least they operate in the same neighborhood as the Were Authority warehouse, and yes, said mysterious business owns at least three properties that are near the ocean."

David flops back on the bed. "Well, isn't that convenient."

"What time is it?" I ask. My head has begun to ache, as if the spell that's blocking Jacques has wrapped my mind in cotton.

"About eight." David stretches, giving me a peek of skin above his shiny silver waistband.

"So we have time to check out the houses on the water."

Rolling onto his side, David curls around me. "*We* can't go anywhere, because the ward is supposed to be portable, but I'm not sure how well it'll work if we're driving around."

"So maybe you two should stay here and I'll go," Connor says.

David's grumbling protest spurs mine. "I don't like that. I'm not going to hang out here where it's relatively safe while you take all the risks."

Connor stares at the ceiling, like he won't have to argue with what he can't see, but there's no way I'm going to let him avoid this discussion.

"I'm with Tray on this one," David says, flopping around until he's propped on his elbows. "I should go with you."

"The two of you aren't leaving me here."

"Brodie." Connor's patting the air like he can calm us down from a distance. "Brodie's in town. I'll ask him to come with me and you two can stay here."

"And do what?" David sounds skeptical.

"Keep digging into the connection between Frank's Magic Warehouse and any American Were Authority businesses that might have dealings with him. Poole restored my access to the Securitas intranet so you can use my computer."

"I still don't like this," I say, embarrassed by how petulant I sound.

"I know, *mo shíorghrá*. I don't either." Connor reaches out as if he's going to caress me, then lets his hand drop. "We'll figure things out. We will."

I'm not sure if he's trying to convince me or himself, but I let it go.

Connor's friend Brodie arrives within the hour. He's a lanky thing with straw-colored dreadlocks and a smile that's more of a leer. Connor once said Brodie is half djinn, and I have no trouble believing that. The djinn play by their own rules, and my respect for Colonel Poole—a man I'm barely acquainted with—rises.

Anyone who can keep a djinn in line must be an excellent leader.

They go off to have adventures while David and I stay behind. David's absorbed in Connor's laptop and I'm swimming through a well of self-pity when my phone beeps. I check it, in case Connor's sent me a text, but it's a number I don't recognize.

Trajan Gall, it has come to our attention that you're interested in meeting with Madame Delia Packard. If that is so, respond to this message.

"Well, damn," I say, mostly to myself.

David looks over. "What?"

"*Madame* Delia Packard is interested in meeting with me." I emphasize the *madame* because who is she kidding? From what I knew, she started life in London's Spitalfields stew. The only madams there ran the brothels and molly houses.

"Isn't that one of the sires Connor and I were going to meet with?"

"Yeah," I say, distracted because I'm trying to figure out how to respond. "Your message must have gotten garbled because she contacted me directly."

"Tell her Connor and I will meet with her tomorrow night."

"Or I can just go now." David's lips thin and I can almost see his arguments building. "You don't play bait and switch with a vampire sire, puppy. She messaged me, so I'm going to go."

"Not alone."

He speaks with conviction, the alpha making a decision rather than my boyfriend offering to help. I have a brief and intense internal debate, then send a response.

Where can we meet you?

I don't explain who *we* is, because that would involve another level of negotiation and I'm not in the mood. They don't make me wait for a response.

Madame Packard has taken a private room at Musso and Frank. Please arrive promptly in one hour.

I relay the message to David, who immediately panics.

"My hair!" He shuts down Connor's computer and darts into the bathroom. I sort through the stuff in my suitcase, looking for something that won't show the wrinkles. Given the volume of curses coming from the wolf, he's having an equally challenging time.

Despite the cursing, he looks good when he's done. I give him a long up and down look, taking in everything from his artfully messy hair to the fit of his distressed jeans. "I'd rather stay here and strip all that off you, puppy."

He crosses the room, moving deliberately, and stops when he's close enough to touch. "Tony, Tony, Tony. If we had more time, you'd be welcome to do just that." He stretches up so I can kiss him. "But let's get the drama handled first."

Grabbing another quick kiss, I agree. "Let's get it over with."

I let David deal with the Uber while I figure out a strategy. Delia Packard is older than Jacques but not old enough to terrify me. We'd met before, but it's not like we ever sat down for a heart-to-heart. Vampires don't do that. From what I know, though, Madame Packard doesn't talk a lot and she's not needlessly cruel. Still, waltzing in with a "How do I break up with Jacques?" is likely to get me killed on principle. On the other hand, I've really got no other reason for reaching out to her.

It might have been smarter to send Connor and David.

In the end I decide that unless Madame Packard asks me point blank what I want, I'll let her do the talking and see what I can learn.

Turns out our hotel isn't that far from the Musso and Frank Grill, which is a good thing because Jacques never shuts up and by the time we reach the restaurant, I'm ready for a straitjacket.

The neon sign out front says the restaurant has been there since 1919, and I can believe it. The vibe inside is heavy on the old school glamour, with red leather booths, polished brass, and trim waiters in bow ties. I drop Madame Packard's name, and the maître d' leads us through the house to a small room off to one side.

The private room's walls are lined with bottles of wine and there's a table in the center covered with a white linen tablecloth. Two open bottles of red wine are on the table and Madame Packard sits across from the door with her back to the corner. She's wearing a midnight velvet jacket over a silk blouse that shows off her pale skin and her deep red lips.

David and I stop just inside the door, waiting to see what kind of greeting we get. Packard's presence must block Jacques and my ears ring with the sudden silence. A man and a woman sit at the table with her. Both vampires. Both staring at us like we've grown an extra head or two.

"Who's your friend?" the man asks. He's sitting on Madame's right, so not a junior varsity player.

"This is David Collins." I address Madame Packard, ignoring the rest. "Thank you for seeing us on short notice."

Madame Packard nods in acknowledgement but doesn't invite us to sit. "Mostly I was curious. Why would Jacques Betancourt's right hand want to talk to me?"

Right hand? "You flatter me."

Her dark eyes assess me to an uncomfortable degree. "I've known Betancourt for a long time, and he's always made a point of saying how much he appreciates your loyalty, how he relies on you to do anything he asks."

I don't respond, although a human would have been blushing with shame. That description makes me sound like a puppet.

"Interesting. You don't like that." Madame Packard leans back in her chair and her associates alternate between watching her and watching me. David moves close enough that I can feel the vibration of his growl against my arm.

"I owe Jacques a great deal."

"Do you?"

Her gaze strips me bare and I realize too late that she must have some level of psychic ability. Which gives me an idea. Maybe she can figure out what I want without me saying the words out loud. Plausible deniability and all.

"I owe him what any scion owes their maker." *Although surely I've paid off my debt by now.*

"Hmm. Yes. I would think so."

She could be agreeing with either my words or my thoughts, or both.

"Have you created any children of your own?" she asks with an appraising tilt of her chin. "You could, you know."

"No, I haven't."

"Maybe you should. A vampire who's strong enough to create others enjoys a greater level of freedom."

"Is that why you won't let me make a child?" the vampire on the right asks. He's a bulky presence with a thick shadow of a beard.

Madame Packard puts a hand on his forearm. "I won't let you make a child because you have the most appalling taste in friends. You'll thank me when you're not stuck for centuries with an utter imbecile."

The bearded vampire's gaze is hot enough to burn holes in the tablecloth, but he doesn't otherwise respond.

David clears his throat, drawing everyone's attention. "So, if Trajan creates another vampire, he'll be free of Jacques?"

Madame Packard's eyes flick over David, her smile growing. "It's not quite that easy, but it will help. Otherwise, you'll just have to kill him. If that's what you want, I mean."

A heavy silence descends. The odds that rumors will spread about this meeting are astronomically high unless Madame Packard has complete control over her scions.

And her grin hints that she wouldn't stop them from talking, even if she could.

Which means that we've walked into a trap. Madame Packard must have known what we want and now she's made sure Jacques will know, too.

Fuck.

"I appreciate your willingness to meet with us, but we won't disturb you any longer." I take hold of David's arm, easing us toward the door.

"But wait." Madame Packard leans forward. "Gillian." She raises a finger, and the woman on her left stands. "My daughter has a favor to ask."

The woman Gillian approaches. She's the curvy maternal sort and she's got her hands clasped tight in front of her belly. "Madame Packard says if she turns my lover, we'll end up hating each other because vampire siblings never get along. Would you please? Dominic is a good man, and he'll make a good vampire."

"I meant to approach Betancourt directly to ask for your services," Madame Packard says, "but since you asked to see me, the timing seemed fortuitous."

I honestly don't know what to say. In all my long years, no one has ever made such a request of me. Creating a vampire child means I'll have an eternity of responsibility, and I have no idea if I'm strong enough to do it. If I'm not strong enough, I'll destroy both of us.

And if I am successful, Jacques won't tolerate the threat. He'll see to it that both the child and I die.

Madame Packard's bitter sidekick will make sure to spread the word of our visit and her offer to turn a human is the definition of a double-edged sword.

She's playing a game and I need to get David out of here before we both lose.

CHAPTER NINE

Okay, so what have you got?" Brodie asks. He's driving and I'm playing copilot.

His ride is a 1970 Malibu sedan with a V8 engine and no airbags. I wouldn't miss them except he drives like a damned maniac.

"I'm not sure." I scroll through the addresses on my list and the one thing they all have in common is their location. They might be on the beach, but my maps app says they all sit elbow to elbow with their neighbors. "If you're a vampire planning something nefarious, you wouldn't do it in front of an audience."

Bodie nods, his aura glowing green with streaks of silver. He'd been the closest thing I had to a friend on the Elites, and while the guy could drive me crazy, tonight he's behaving.

"What about some of the non-beach addresses?"

"But the Princess said…" I let the thought trail. Yeah, maybe I'd had a spiritual interaction with the Princess Tatiana, or maybe it was a lie like all the other lies we'd heard at the viscount's place.

We'd wasted time driving past one of the houses in Redondo Beach, which made the error in our thinking obvious. The address was on a stretch of road where a person could stand between any two houses and touch them both at the same time. Jacques may own the place, but he's not hiding the Princess there.

I go back to the maps app and see what else I can come up with. "Hey, there's a house up in the hills over Malibu that looks like it doesn't have any close neighbors."

"That sounds more like it."

I plug the address into the GPS and suppress a groan when it says it's going to take an hour and a half to get there. It's a little after three a.m., and while neither Brodie nor I have the sunrise hard stop a vampire does, I'd still like to be home before Trajan retires.

I want to see him, to know he's okay, even if I can't touch him.

We're on surface streets for the time being, which gives us even more opportunity to get bored with each other.

"Just like old times, yeah Mack?"

Brodie's question startles me and I wonder if he somehow knows what's going on in my head. "Which part? The long drive or the bad jokes?"

"Hardee har."

He's driving a good ten miles over the speed limit but I don't bother to point it out because it'll only make him go faster.

"Do you miss it? The Elites, I mean?"

Brodie sounds semi-serious so I give my answer about the same amount of consideration. "Not sure. Can't say I miss the adrenaline rush of a job when we've been moving every day or so to keep ahead of Jacques."

"That's crazy."

"It's exhausting, is what it is. I want to find that asshole vampire and do whatever it takes to keep him from hurting Trajan."

Brodie's steering with two fingers at six o'clock and again I keep my mouth shut. He'll only drive faster. He's a djinn. He can't help it.

"Keep him from hurting Trajan or keep him from killing you? Seems like that ought to be your priority."

I laugh because duh. "It's a two-birds-with-one-stone deal."

"Interesting metaphor."

"Hey, you used a three-syllable word!" I grin out the window, waiting for the eff-bomb.

"Fuck you, Mack."

"Oh please. I've got enough dick in my life."

He exaggerates a laugh, pounding the steering wheel. "Who knew you were such a freak."

Laughing, I wave him off. He guides the old car onto the freeway, the big engine rumbling.

"You don't even ask about our jobs." Brodie sounds uncharacteristically serious. "I can't decide if it's because you really want to forget, or if you miss us too bad to talk about us."

I brush a lank strand of hair out of my face, wondering if he can see my blush. "It's not that I don't want to hear about your cases and all. I've just had my hands full."

"Yeah, with a dick in each one. I get it."

I shake my head, stifling a flinch when he changes lanes and cuts somebody off. "You could use your turn signal."

He changes lanes again, this time earning a honk from another driver. His smile is full of false innocence. "Say what?"

While he's watching me, he's bearing down on a Honda who probably shouldn't be in the high-speed lane, but I grind my teeth rather than pointing it out to him.

"Tell me about your last case." I spit the words out and he taps the brakes, managing to avoid rear-ending the Honda.

"You would have had fun. Spent a week in Cuba exorcising an old church and eating the best damned food you could imagine. They do incredible things with bananas."

"Bananas? You usually lead with the pretty girls."

"Oh yeah. The ladies were lovely, as were some of the gents."

I side-eye him. "You changing teams?"

"Let's just say I'm keeping my options open."

That pretty much exhausts my conversational arsenal. I could ask him if he's got any upcoming plans, but with the Elites, you know where you're going when Poole sends you your flight information. That's one of the things I don't miss. Being on the run with David and Trajan is challenging, but at least we have some control over our time.

We ride on in silence. Brodie fiddles with the stereo, which is clearly a lot newer than the car. He finds a station playing salsa and we meander up the 405, getting to know our neighbors.

Because yes, there's traffic even at three a.m.

We go from the freeway to the Pacific Coast Highway to a smaller surface street to what appears to be a gravel road. There's a turn-out a couple hundred yards from where the maps app says the house should be, and even though we haven't seen it yet, we leave the car and go forward on foot.

We'll attract less attention that way.

The house seems to rise up from its surroundings like a natural creation of wood and glass and stone. A handful of windows are lit from within, and when we get close enough, Brodie tosses a stone toward the corner of the house. It's not a lot of motion, but enough to turn the light on.

"Hmph," he grunts, and we share a glance. I motion toward one direction and point him in the other, figuring we can circle the perimeter and meet up on the other side.

He takes off and so do I, keeping to the edge of the lawn so I don't trigger any of the lights. Not sure how we're going to get inside, but we'll deal with that later.

The opposite side of the house overlooks Malibu and, further out, the Pacific. I get there before Brodie does. On this side the lawn is terraced, with a paved trail leading to an infinity pool on the next level, and beyond that…

Beyond that I find Brodie, wrestling with a guy in a classic black tux. They're well-matched in height, though Brodie's opponent is broader. Even so, what Brodie lacks in size he makes up for in crazy. Tux has hold of a gun, Brodie has hold of Tux's wrist, and neither is going to give up.

And Brodie's laughing. Because of course he is. He tries a head-butt and Tux's dress shoes slide on the sand, but he quickly scrambles back into the fight.

Pulling my own pistol out of its holster, I aim it at Tux.

"Don't move," I say.

"Don't you move." A voice, along with the sensation of a gun's muzzle against my neck, freeze me in place.

"Enough, Leander. Let him go." The person behind me jams the gun deeper into my neck. "This is the one we want."

I share a glance with Brodie. He's still got ahold of Tux's wrist, although the starch has gone out of their fight. He raises his eyebrows and I swallow hard. On a mental count of three, I shift.

Instead of Connor, I'm a big, black dog.

At the same time, Brodie sets off a smoke bomb of some kind—his specialty and I don't ask too many questions—and in the heartbeat it takes our opponents to adjust, we run full-tilt around the house and back down the gravel drive.

I get to the car before he does, and I've shifted by the time he arrives. We get in and he puts that big V8 to work, hauling ass down the winding road toward the Pacific Coast Highway.

Neither of us says anything until we're a good two miles away.

"You okay?" I ask. Whatever was tying Brodie's dreads out of his face got lost in the fight and they're hanging heavy over his shoulders. There's a scuff mark on one cheekbone, like maybe he caught part of a punch, and there's a new hole in the knee of his jeans.

"Just like old times, man. Fuck, we weren't even doing anything."

"Maybe not, but I think we figured out where the vampire is hiding." *This is the one we want.* The words are on constant loop in my head. How did they know? "They must have security cameras set up all along the driveway."

Waves be damned. We'd definitely found the vampire's hide-out.

Now we just had to figure out what to do with that information.

CHAPTER TEN

How the hell long is a fortnight?" I mean, just because the lady vampire learned English in the nineteenth century doesn't mean she has to show it off.

The vampire in question, some supposedly badass vampire sire, is doing a fine Morticia Addams imitation, with a grin that came straight off Uncle Fester.

And she's apparently just handed Trajan a golden ticket, except I trust her about as much as I'd trust Fester. There's gotta be a catch.

"A fortnight, young cub, is fourteen days," the Morticia wanna-be says. Her name is technically Delia, but I like calling her Morticia. It reminds me that despite looking like a human cartoon character, she is dangerous.

"You'll do it, then?" Gillian, a vampire who looks like she'd be happier baking a batch of cookies than draining someone, gives Trajan an earnestly hopeful look.

Puh-lease.

"We'll turn it into a party." Morticia grins at us from the head of the table. I smile back, my wolf simmering right along the surface of my skin.

My wolf's been agitated ever since the restaurant's host trapped us in a wine room with Madame Packard with no obvious way out. Trajan's not a lot calmer than I am, his tension winding my wolf up further.

"I would be honored to assist you in this way." Trajan speaks in measured tones at odds with the energy zinging between us. "Although I am unsure whether I'm up to the task."

"And I'm unsure whether it's a good idea in the first place," I mumble, earning a sharp look from Madame Packard. Trajan nudges me with his elbow which I take to mean *stfu before you make things worse.*

"In my present circumstances, I'd be unable to provide the care a new scion would require."

And if getting away from Jacques were that easy, you would have known how already.

Madame Morticia Packard waves off Trajan's concerns. "Once the man is turned, I'll assume responsibility for him since he'll be bonded with Gillian."

Trajan doesn't respond, and while what I know about vampires would fit in a microchip, it's all I can do not to poke hard at her plan.

"That's very gracious of you," Trajan says. "I'd like to be allowed to think this over."

Madame Packard raises a quizzical eyebrow. "So you can discuss it with Jacques? I don't think so."

The finality in the vampire sire's tone makes it clear that our only way out of here is if Trajan agrees to turn Gillian's boyfriend into a vampire.

Sweet. Let's just put ourselves into the worst possible circumstances.

Trajan inhales deeply, then nods in Gillian's direction. "I will do it, then."

"In blood." Madame Packard rises, producing a stiletto from somewhere.

Without a glance at me, Trajan walks toward the table. I want to stop him. My wolf *really* wants to stop him, but it seems like our only way out is through.

Trajan stops when he's at the head of the table. He holds out his hand, and the vampire sire makes a slice across his palm. She makes a similar cut in her own palm, and they clasp hands.

Something heavy falls over us, a blanket of sand that makes it hard to breathe. Trajan and Madame Packard stare at each other, as if they're engaged in a conversation we can't hear.

And then it's done. They release their grip, the sand blanket goes away, and Trajan slowly returns to my side.

If his skin was any paler, he'd be invisible.

"Prepare yourself, Mr. Gall, and notify me when you are ready." Her voice has taken on a deeper resonance, as if the power from whatever spell she just worked still flows through her. Trajan nods, his back to her. He reaches for my hand, and together, we leave them to their dinner. Or wine. Or whatever it is they're doing in a fancy-ass restaurant.

Or maybe the maître d' has a trio of virgins waiting for them in the storage pantry. I don't even know.

The ride back to our hotel doesn't help much. In addition to being pale, Trajan goes silent, but it's the kind of tortured silence that makes me wonder what's really going on in his head.

"Did you know about the whole *turn someone into a vampire and break free of your maker* thing?" I pose the question because I want to know but also because I want to make sure he's still with me on some level.

He waits long enough that I decide he's not going to answer at all when he snarls, "Not in so many words."

Uh, okay. "You knew—"

"I knew that turning a human entailed access to power, and that successful completion of the act would give a vampire greater independence. But…" He cracks his knuckles, one hand at a time. "I did not expect to possess the level of power required."

His voice breaks on the end, giving me a glimpse of a wound I'd never suspected. "You didn't think you had the power, or Jacques didn't let you know about it?"

"Shut up. Do not say his name."

I blink, once, because I've seen Trajan in all sorts of moods, but never…mean. Like, I have to talk myself down from a sudden shift because my wolf feels so threatened. Thank the sweet baby Jesus we're almost at the hotel. I gotta hope the ward helps Trajan calm down.

Either that or things are going to get ugly.

The walk from the Uber to the hotel room is about ten miles long. Not really, but it feels that way. I keep a hand on Trajan in case he wanders off in a cloud of his own distress, swipe the keycard on the door, and almost shove him inside.

"Where's Connor?" His question comes through clenched teeth.

"He's probably still out with Brodie. They were going to check the houses along the coast."

Trajan stands still in the middle of the floor. He doesn't take his coat off, doesn't rake the hank of hair that's fallen into his face. His hands are fisted and I start to get nervous. He's not calming down. Has the ward's power faded already?

I'd left it on the nightstand on "my" side of the bed, but when I glance over, it's gone.

Gone.

Shit.

Nothing else seems out of place. My bag is still half-open on the floor and the door to Trajan's room is shut.

Wait. Was it shut before?

I slide over, worried that anything I do might provoke him. Between whatever Jacques is doing to him and the pact with Delia Packard, my big vampire is hanging by a thread. Slowly, I open the door.

Chaos.

Someone has tossed his room. Clothing is strewn everywhere and there's a picture...a picture...

On the center of his pillow, there's a black and white photograph of a man. He's young, maybe twenty, and he's posed facing the camera, wearing a white button-down shirt. Only a shirt. His cock hangs below the white fabric between his spread legs, and while he's not smiling, there's an invitation in his eyes.

It's Trajan.

A younger version, skinny enough to be called bony, his greasy hair hanging over one eye, but it's definitely him. Looking closer, I see someone has torn this photograph in pieces, then put them back together.

What the hell?

Without giving it a whole lot of thought, I grab my phone and start a text to Connor.

Don't come back here. Something's really wrong and I'm afraid –

The door to our suite opens before I can hit send. After one last glance at the photograph, I head toward the sounds of a fight.

Trajan has Connor pinned against the desk, his hands around Conor's throat. Connor's Elite buddy Brodie is the one making all the noise. He's got a pistol against Trajan's temple and a maniac's grin.

"Don't…Brodie, don't." Connor manages to rasp out the words. He's got ahold of Trajan's wrists, but as strong as he is, he's no match for the vampire. His face is bright red, his nostrils flared.

Fuck. I've got exactly one option. "Brodie, drop the gun."

With those words, I shift.

Rage has a scent that's uglier than the stink of fear. Madness is worse than both. I growl at Brodie, who does the smart thing and moves out of my way. Baring my fangs, I lunge toward Trajan, latching onto the meatiest part of his thigh.

He swings around, tearing himself out of my jaw. I'm faced with the vampire, eyes wholly black, nothing remotely human in his expression. His fangs are long, nearly to his chin, and *Oh fuck this is going to hurt.*

I leap at him before he can get me trapped against the bed. He yields a step and I snap at him and miss. My wolf knows I must force the danger out. I leap at him again, this time tearing a chunk out of his hand. He moves back another step. Connor's making word-shaped noises that I don't understand. His friend is gone.

Trajan comes at me and I rise up on my hind legs, meeting him with claws and teeth. He tries to grab my throat but I slice at him and he gives way. Maybe there's still something human in there, and maybe that little bit of humanity recognizes me because he's holding back despite the blood I've drawn.

We seesaw back and forth, with me doing my best to edge Trajan toward the door. I lunge, fatigue catching up to me, but this time he doesn't move.

He can't. There's someone behind him, someone with an unnaturally long arm that stretches around his chest, pinning him in place.

Someone holding a hypodermic needle that he's jabbed into Trajan's neck.

One long moment later, Trajan sags. Brodie catches him before he can hit the floor.

I sit back on my haunches, breathing hard. Connor comes over and kneels in front of me. He threads his fingers through my ruff and I swear there are tears in his eyes. "Thank you, David."

I nod because that's all I can do. When he stands, I shift. Connor and Brodie hoist Trajan onto the bed, and I supervise from my bare-assed perch on the floor.

"I would have texted you, but you got here too soon." My voice holds onto the wolf's growl.

"It's okay, *mo mhuirnin*. If you hadn't been here, things would have turned out a lot worse."

Connor holds out his hand and I grasp it, letting him do most of the work involved with getting me to my feet. I've got bruises in places I didn't know could bruise and there's a patch on my shoulder where Trajan's fingernails clawed me.

Trajan. I drop onto the edge of the bed, covering his cold hand with mine. "Someone stole the ward and they trashed the vampire room."

"*Damnú.*"

Connor caresses my shoulder and I tilt my head so I can rub my cheek against his knuckles.

Brodie's got a black case open on the dresser. "Want me to give him another hit? I'm not sure how long that one will last."

"Not yet," Connor says. "Lemme see his room."

He's got his hand on the door to the vampire room when I bleat, "Connor, wait. There's something in there, something he wouldn't want us to see."

Connor scowls and the flash of anger that washes over him makes me blink. Without another word, he heads into the vampire room.

A muttered curse tells me he's found the photograph.

He comes through the door and heads straight for his laptop bag. He's wearing all black, same as Brodie, and it accentuates the lines of his body.

And OMG did I really just have a lusty thought after shifting and fighting off my enraged vampire boyfriend? JFC, David Collins.

When Connor straightens, his expression is on the far side of grim, almost too angry. "We can assume from all this that Jacques knows where we're staying."

"Unless some rando decided to trash Tray's room and take the one thing that gave him any peace." Bitterness bleeds through my words.

Brodie picks up another syringe. "You sure?" he asks Connor.

"Nah, don't worry about it." Connor comes over and stands next to me. "You can take off. I've got it from here."

Connor's whiskey and leather scent comforts me, and so does the syringe Brodie leaves on the dresser. He gives Connor a semi-mocking salute, and then it's just the two of us.

Well, the three of us if you count our unconscious boyfriend.

"Did you have any luck finding Jacques?"

"Yeah." Connor puts his hands on my shoulders and starts to rub. When he finishes his story about the house in the hills over Malibu, I tell him about Delia Packard and the pact Trajan agreed to.

"*Dia á sábháil.* There's no coming back from something like that."

Trajan stirs, and I barely keep from flinching. "What are we going to do, Connor?"

"I don't—"

"Let me go." Trajan, his eyes bleary but human, struggles to prop himself up on his elbows. "Let me go, *amore mio*, before I hurt both of you."

I leap up, ready to shift if I need to, every muscle in my body bitching to high hell over the idea. Connor reaches for Trajan but I block him, because *no fucking way* are we going to invite catastrophe.

Trajan manages to sit and then, vampire quick, he's standing. "I have to prepare myself for what Madame Packard has asked of me, and until then, it's too dangerous for me to be around you. Please." He closes his eyes, grimacing like he's fighting down the worst pain. "Please let me go."

Then he's gone, torn jacket, uncombed hair, and all.

And Connor and I stare at each other like we don't know what the fuck to do next.

Part Two: Different Roads.
Same Goal

CHAPTER ELEVEN

Trajan

Not so long ago, I was ready to walk into the sun. I had reached a point where this life I've led for some one hundred fifty years no longer seemed worth the effort. Then I met a wolf named David, and he convinced me to give it one more try. Then Connor returned from the dead, and I had another reason to live.

But Jacques Betancourt would have me destroy everything that had given me hope. And for what? To prove I am his dog, that I'll come when he says come and fetch when he says fetch.

And to kill when he says kill.

No. This time he's pushed me too far. I will not kill Connor, even if it means I must face the sun myself.

So, grasping at the little spell of sanity before Jacques' voice resumes its awful chant, I leave the hotel where we've been hiding—although since David's magic hacky sack has been stolen, we haven't been all that well hidden.

I stride through the darkness, fumbling with my phone. David's usually in charge of organizing Ubers, but I do have the app. I arrange for a pick-up; my destination is Stone's warehouse, where I've parked my Land Rover. My plan is to make my way to the Ten, and from there head for the desert.

The town of Joshua Tree is small, but they used to have a hotel with vampire-ready rooms. Twentynine Palms is bigger and not much further east. I'd once had to stake out a Chupacabra who'd lost a poker game with Jacques, then tried to run out on his debt.

Chasing a goat sucker in human form through any town is enough to turn you off to a place.

Further east is more desert, and while I can admit destroying myself might be necessary, I'm not ready to give in yet.

So I settle on Joshua Tree and ride out on a wave of crazy. Jacques is back in my head, cajoling and ordering and generally making me want to drive a stake through his heart. The further I go, though, the quieter he gets.

Thankful for small blessings, I turn off my phone and drive on in the darkness.

The LA sprawl goes on and on, and some two hours after leaving my lovers, I turn onto Highway 62. The sky is huge and studded with stars. There are no streetlights out this far, but my night vision is more than up to the task. I pass shadowy stands of windmills, shrubby scrub, and, finally, the tortured silhouettes of the trees that give the place its name.

The town of Joshua Tree hugs the highway and the cross streets don't travel very far before they fade into gravel and dirt. The population is low, although a continuous stream of tourists visiting the national park gives the town a reason to exist.

I park in front of the High Desert Motel, a two-story walk-up with white walls and a red roof. The office is lit up like Christmas, as if the owners are afraid late-night guests will need blinking colored lights to find their way in.

Since my phone is turned off, I don't know what time it is, but I'd guess two a.m. Jacques' litany of commands is a distant drum beat; if I think about the number of stars or the heavy desert silence, I barely hear him. I already miss David and Connor, a tiny pinprick of pain that also acts as a distraction.

One way or the other, I'll keep Jacques out.

The woman at the front desk snarls when I walk in. She's greasy in a way that feels deliberate and the place stinks of wolf. Maybe she's hiding a passel of packmates somewhere. "Evening." I keep my voice calm and my hands visible. "I'm wondering if you've got a vampire room available."

The snarl turns into a laugh. "You got a permit?"

And *now* she's fucking with me. "Nope."

She shrugs her bony shoulders. "Place this small, we can't have some random bloodsucker waltzing in and expecting a free meal."

"You're big enough to have a hospital. If I stay long enough, I'll see about some expired blood from their blood bank."

Her lips curl the way mine want to. "Gross."

"Coming from someone who smells like an unwashed wolves' den, I'll take that under advisement."

She raises both hands like she wants me to back off. "No need to get nasty."

I shrug. "So do you have a vampire room or not?" There are a few more places I could try, but I've stayed here before so I know they'll have what I need.

A windowless room, a bed, and a door that locks.

"I told you, no permit, no room."

"Then I'll try someplace else."

"Won't matter. No permit, no room. City ordinance."

"Twentynine Palms?"

"You'll need a permit there, too."

She stares at me with just enough of a smirk that I still think she's fucking with me. "Good night. Thanks for nothing."

I turn to go and about the time I get my hand on the door, she says, "Wait. I know where there's a cave."

I glance at her over my shoulder. "Does it smell like wolves?"

"Nah." She scratches behind her ear and I imagine she has fleas, too. "It's about a two mile hike, and it's deep enough to keep you out of the sun."

"Does it have a door that locks?"

That makes her laugh. "Shoulda done your homework, dude."

I give her a mocking salute and head for the Range Rover. I try the Best Western Joshua Tree and the Joshua Tree Inn, and a couple other places whose names I can't remember. They all give me the same bullshit about a permit. In theory I have time to make it back to LA, but the closer I get to home, the louder Jacques' voice gets, so I decide to see a wolf about a cave.

When I come back through the office door, the clerk laughs so hard I'm afraid she's going to rupture something. I cross the room and plant both hands on the counter, waiting till she's at the gasping for breath stage to speak.

"So, can you tell me where the cave is?"

"For fifty dollars," she wheezes.

Gritting my teeth, I ask, "Can you break a twenty?"

"Oh, did I say fifty? I meant sixty."

If she didn't smell so bad I'd be tempted to drain her on principle. She must see it in my eyes, because her laughter dries up and she waves me toward the back of the room.

"Come this way. I can't leave the desk long enough to take you there, but I'll show you the trail."

She takes me out a rear door and points up the road running behind the motel. "Follow that past the last house and you'll see a path. There's a big-ass Joshua tree right where it starts. Follow it for a couple miles, and every time it forks, go left. The cave'll be on the hill side by a big saguaro cactus. I'd say you can't miss it, but you totally can, so pay attention."

This is sounding sketchier by the minute, as David would say, but I don't have much choice. Taking directions from the flea-bitten desk clerk of a fleabag motel, I hope to hell I'm not piling more trouble on my head.

"But he won't really die," she says, her voice layered with a resonance she didn't have before. "You'll think you killed him, but the stars say you're wrong."

"What?"

She blinks at me, like she's just waking up. "No need to get pissy. I just—"

It's all I can do not to close my hand around her throat. "You just said that he wouldn't really die. Who the hell were you talking about?"

"Oh." She laughs weakly and wave a hand toward the trail. "Just ignore me when I go off like that. My brain is weird."

My glare isn't drawing anything else out of her, so I shrug and leave it for later. Either she's referring to Jacques or to Connor or to a victim-to-be-named later. None of those options give me a whole lot of hope.

She runs through the directions one more time and I take off up the road. I aim for about a three-minute mile pace, slow enough that I won't miss anything. Her instructions are accurate; I pass the houses, find the trailhead by the Joshua tree, pick the left branch of every fork.

I make my best guess at a mile and a half and slow down so I won't miss the cave's entrance. Still, I almost jog right past the saguaro cactus, because the cave I think I'm looking for is big and black and the reality is more like a crevice between tumbled rocks. *She didn't tell me about the rocks.*

Still, I like that it's hidden and I like the lack of footprints. Anybody who wants to rob me while I'm down for the day will have to know just where they're going.

And if anybody does rob me, I'll know to start looking at a certain werewolf/front desk clerk.

Worming my way through the rocks, I find the entrance to the cave. It's large enough that even my sight can't penetrate the darkness. *Good.*

I'd left LA without my overnight case, so I don't have anything remotely like a mattress or even a pillow. There's no water to wash, and while I'm not truly hungry, if a certain bleached-blond werewolf was around, I'd probably have a snack.

But David's not here and neither is Connor. In the darkness of the cave, I have to focus to hear Jacques. *Small blessings, man.* I poke around in the darkness, feeling my way along the wall of the cave until I work my way back to the entrance.

"Well, Trajan Gall, you've done it this time."

Somehow I hear my mother's voice, and it makes me flinch. Mother had a good heart and a fierce temper. She sang opera whenever she could find a production, but along the

Mississippi during the War Between the States, there weren't many singing jobs to be had.

So she took other work, the kind that ate her soul as surely as the consumption ate her lungs.

"Enough." I shake myself. Making my way to the deepest part of the cave, I prop myself against the wall. The darkness hasn't changed, but sunrise is close. I barely have time to fret over what it'll take to turn a human when my mind goes dark.

After that I don't worry about anything.

CHAPTER TWELVE

Step one is finding a new place to stay, ideally one Betancourt doesn't know about. Step two is finding Trajan. And step three? Navigating vampire politics to keep Trajan safe and all of us alive.

Simple. Shouldn't be a problem at all.

I suck at sarcasm.

"This place is okay," David says, although his nose is ever so slightly wrinkled. His wolf's nose picks up more than I do, but I find I'm not interested in whatever died in this hotel room.

"We can move on in a day or so."

"We might not need to. I mean, we're hiding from Betancourt, who seems to be tracking Trajan, not us."

"Yeah, but if we move again, we can be pickier about where we stay."

"Sure. Next time we can find someplace on the upside of decent."

"Let's not get carried away."

He laughs, and for a minute everything's okay. But only for a minute.

David and I are in a Motel 6 south of LAX. With faux-hardwood floors and an incongruous orange wall, it's not fancy. But since we called to reserve a room at midnight, I'm just glad the door locks.

"We should probably try to grab some sleep," I say.

David's expression sobers. "I keep telling myself that he's been a vampire for a lot longer than I can imagine, so I should trust him to be able to take care of himself."

I cross the room — it's small enough that I cover the distance in two steps — and take hold of his shoulder. He's so tight I start massaging without really paying attention to what I'm doing.

"Hey. Stop." David jerks away from me. "This isn't the time to get romantic."

I stand there with my jaw around my knees. "I just...your muscles are tight...I'm sorry if I overstepped."

He spins away from me, one hand raised like he's putting up a wall between us.

"I didn't mean to upset you."

David doesn't move, so I do, coming closer to him than is probably wise. He's so stiff I think I've made a mistake, but then he sighs, his body melting against mine.

"No, I'm sorry, Connor. I'm just so worried about him."

I wrap an arm across his chest. "Me too, *mo mhuirnin*. Me too."

"We should have gone after him."

I hug him tighter. "We did, David. He can move faster than either of us and if he doesn't want to be found, we won't find him."

He mumbles something, and at my "What?" he rubs his cheek on my shoulder.

"You get to call Sheena this time. I had to call her the time he got shot."

I nuzzle his hair, enjoying the light perfume of his product. "Might be worth asking her where he'd go to hide out."

His laugh vibrates against my chest. "Yeah, and after we recover from the beatdown she gives us, we can go looking for him."

We untangle from each other, and I go for my phone. "Text or phone call?"

"You may as well call her. If you text *'Trajan is missing – where should we look?'* she'll call you to chew you out."

"Right." I check the time. Two a.m. If she had a bodyguarding gig, she's probably home already, and if she was at The Club, they're shutting down. I gather my cojones and swipe the screen.

"What?"

Sheena answers so abruptly I almost drop the phone. "Everything okay?"

"No. Everything's not okay. You're calling me in the middle of the damned night, which means you either found another body somewhere or Trajan's been injured in some way. Now talk."

She must be at The Club. She's got her Domme voice on, and she's loud, as if she's been talking over a disco beat. David rolls his eyes from his perch on the bed. He must hear her too.

"Trajan left. Where would he go?"

"Left? What do you mean?"

I massage the muscles in my neck. "Over the last week or so, Jacques has been putting the screws to him. Like, Jacques showed up at one of the VRBOs where we were staying, or at least his spirit did. Things got worse tonight and Trajan took off, saying he…" I tried to remember Trajan's exact words. "He said it was too dangerous for him to be around us."

"And you let him go?" Her voice is flat, menacing, and all of a sudden, I'm out of patience.

"Save it, princess," I snap. "I'm not the enemy. If you have any idea where Trajan might hide out for a couple weeks, let me know. Otherwise, I'll see you when I see you."

"If you'd stayed dead the first time, Trajan wouldn't be having this problem, would he?"

My jaw's so tight I can hear my teeth grind. "If you think of anything helpful, let me know."

"Not until I hear from Trajan myself."

The phone goes dead and I drop it on the bed, my hand limp. David's covering his face with his hands, which I take to mean he thinks I'm out of line. *Whatever.* "Do you need me to recap that?"

David's laugh is muffled. "Um, no. No, I heard it just fine the first time."

I sit on the foot of the bed, my elbows on my knees. After a while, David starts talking. "So next time we have to call Sheena, I'll do it, m'kay?"

I let loose a snort. "Sure."

"I mean, calling her names might not have been your smartest move."

"Look, Sheena wasn't my biggest fan the first time around. I guess tonight I just wasn't in the mood for her attitude."

"Yeah." He reaches a hand toward me. "I get that. She can be a lot."

Clasping his hand, I intertwine my fingers with his. His presence is a comfort, but my mind is still whirring. "I'd also like to know what she can tell us about Trajan's life before he became a vampire."

David sits so we're side by side. "That picture."

"Yeah. It's definitely him, but…"

I can't finish the thought. Trajan had said he'd become a vampire in the early 1870s. "What do we know about the history of photography?"

David nudges me with his shoulder, laughing. "That's what God made Google for."

"Okay, I'll call Stone and see if he knows where Trajan might have gone, and you can look up the history of photography."

"I can just imagine the search terms now. Did they have pornos in the 1800s?"

That makes me laugh, which breaks the chain of tension that's been tightening in my shoulders. "I don't know, *mo mhuirnin*, but I'm sure you'll find out."

CHAPTER THIRTEEN

DAVID

So I wake up with, well, it's not morning wood, because my watch says it's three p.m. But it's wood, anyway. I'd spent a good chunk of the night googling vintage porn. *Who knew the Victorians were so horny?*

I'm curled on my side and Connor's spooned around me. His heavy exhalations flutter through my hair with the hint of a snore. I want to slap myself. No way is this the time to get sexy. With Trajan MIA and Connor dealing with an up close and personal death threat, sex seems highly inappropriate.

But my dick wants what it wants.

My hips wiggle, all on their own, completely disconnected to my mind. They — my hips, which are no longer paying attention to my words — rub in the general vicinity of Connor's cock. He's wearing jeans, so I'm not getting instant feedback, but the rhythm of his breathing changes.

I rub some more, because come on, I'm twenty-three and he's hot. He gives a sharp inhale and his hand clamps down on my hip, dragging me closer.

From here I can feel the ridge of his cock running down one pant leg and I sigh. My wiggle turns into a more direct hip thrust. He slides his hand down my thigh, cupping my dick. I'm naked and already leaking and when he rubs his thumb over my little head, I arch against him.

"Wanna fuck you," he murmurs. He punctuates that statement by rubbing his rough stubble against my shoulder.

"Sounds good to me."

He nips my ear, then manhandles me onto my back, propping my hips with a pillow. His leather and whiskey scent makes my mouth water, and he works silently, as if afraid if he says anything at all the name Trajan will come up and spoil the mood. We'd begun to talk about rules and parameters, until the whole thing with Jacques had us running from one place to the next.

Personal safety outweighs things like jealousy and hurt.

I'm lying there with my ass in the air while Connor strips off his jeans and produces lube from his bag. His intense focus sets off a fluttery feeling in my gut. *Maybe we shouldn't…*

He crouches between my legs, sucking one of my balls into his mouth.

Okay, yeah. We definitely should. We can talk about it later.

With that, I let go and just feel. He's alternating between my balls, sucking on one and then the other, he's stroking my dick, and he's got a finger in my asshole.

"So good, Pookie. So, so good."

He bites my ballsack hard enough to let me know he noticed the pet name. I smile at the ceiling, bones and muscles softening.

All except my dick. It's rock hard and Connor's finger is deep enough in my ass to stroke the spot that sends sensation zinging through me. I start humping in time with his strokes and he chuckles.

"You're so pretty when you let go like this." He slides more lube around my hole. "Usually by this time Trajan's balls-deep in me and I don't have the chance to appreciate you."

Needle scratch. I freeze, looking up at him with my lower lip caught between my teeth.

"What?" He sits back on his heels, loosening his grip on my dick.

"Nothing," I whisper, in that quavery voice that sounds like a lie.

"Do you think Trajan would mind us doing this? Because I don't."

He sounds defensive, as if he's trying to convince himself. I reach down and take hold of his hand, wrapping it tighter around my cock. I take a four-count inhale and let it go more slowly. "I agree with you. He wouldn't mind, and I" — *probably should shut my mouth now* — "really want you inside me."

I must be convincing because in a couple of heartbeats, the head of his cock nudges my hole. He grabs ahold of my thighs, bending me in half.

His first thrust stretches me and I rock my head back so he can't see me wince. It doesn't hurt, exactly, and I really don't want him to stop. It just takes me a minute or two to accommodate his size.

Did I mention he's hung like the horse he can shift into?

He works his way in, and only when his balls slap against my ass does he whisper, "You're a wonder, *mo mhuirnin*. I'm so glad we have each other."

I am too, I want to say, but the words get caught up in the steady rhythm of his thrusts. He fills me, his hands forcing me to bend further till my knees are close to my ears. His rhythm changes, pounding me faster with short, hard strokes, and he lets go of one leg so he can stroke my dick again.

Oh god that's going to undo me. I thrash underneath his onslaught, my head rocking side to side, my hips straining to meet his pace. This feels so damned good. Different than when there are three of us, but it's like comparing filet mignon to prime rib.

They're both fucking delicious.

Connor loses his rhythm and with a growl, he stiffens, his cock so deep in me I can feel it in my throat. I add my hand to his where it's wrapped around my dick, finding the perfect speed and pressure and soon I'm coming, too. Pleasure pulls me up higher than sound and sends me floating slowly to the too-small bed in the odiferous hotel room. Connor's still inside me, but he's softening. He's braced on his elbows so I'm not bearing his full weight.

But if he wanted to lie on me, that'd be okay, too. I'll carry him as far as he needs to go.

After a while, Connor's dick slides out of me. He catches hold of my hands and stretches them up over my head so we're lying belly to belly, forehead to forehead. The moment turns heavy, as if there are things we both want to say but don't.

To make sure we don't, I tip my head so I can kiss him, long and slow. He lets go of one wrist, propping himself on his elbow, taking control. I'm more than happy to let him, and we kiss until I think our spirits are melding and I'm breathing hard.

Connor breaks the kiss, tracing the line of my lower lip with his thumb. "We should probably —"

"Yeah." I interrupt him because if we keep doing what we're doing someone's going to get hurt. "Did you and Brodie cover all of Jacques' beach houses?"

"At least the three we know about. I mean, we're pretty sure he's staying in that house in the hills above Malibu. I can also email Melinda Barwell. She's a Sensitive with Securitas and she may be able to help us narrow our search." He rolls to my side and I drape one leg over his, letting him know we're still connected. In response, he puts a hand on my thigh, because we might have started out linked through Trajan, but we're building bonds of our own, too.

Covering his hand with my own, I pick and choose from a pile of ideas. "I could text Lydia and see if she's heard anything useful. Actually, it might be a good idea to check in with her anyway to see if that Los Feliz pack leader has given her any more shit."

"Sounds good. You shower and I'll see if I can find any houses I might have missed, then I'll shower and you can ping Lydia."

I pout. "But we could shower together."

He pinches my thigh and I thrash to get away from him. "The shower in this place is barely big enough for one of us," he says. "And if we do manage to fit, we'll never want to get out."

The heat in his gaze makes me smile. "True dat. Let's stick with Plan A and we'll see what trouble we can stir up tonight."

"Don't even say that." Rolling his eyes, he climbs out of bed. "We find enough trouble when we're not even looking for it."

He's not wrong. I climb into the shower, and something about the fall of warm water makes me think of that copycat Mirror of Derised that the viscount had in his pretend basement. I'd told Connor I saw the three of us with my sister and Marcus and all, but what I hadn't told him is that we were all in tuxedos — well, except mine was a vintage tailcoat worn with a lace cravat, a blue brocade vest the color of the ocean near the horizon, and knee-high riding boots.

I also didn't tell him that the three of us were holding hands and someone, honestly it might have been Lydia Sanchez, was in front of us with a small black book that looked a lot like a Bible.

Could it be that my secret desire was to get married? Or were they officially appointing me as alpha? I side-eye both options and soap up.

Massaging my scalp to get rid of any leftover product, I'm reluctant to get out of the shower. The water pressure is surprisingly good for an airport hotel and, well, it's nicer in here than whatever I'm about to face. There's no way we're going to find Trajan and get rid of Jacques without a whole lot of sturm and drang, and not the heavy metal kind.

Of course, no one is actively shooting at us, so maybe I should count my blessings and stop being a whiner.

I turn the water off and get dried and dressed as fast as possible. I'm wearing cropped yoga pants and a loose sweatshirt, hoping I can work in some sun salutations between text messages. Connor and I smack hands and yell "Tag" and I find my phone.

I've already got one message, from Sheena. She doesn't sound angry, but then it's hard to judge from *Call me when you get the chance.*

I text Lydia first, saying it's been a while and we should have a chat over the beverage of her choice. Then, with a reasonable amount of trepidation, I dial Sheena's number.

"He's not answering his goddamn phone."

I inhale, sorry I hadn't done some yoga before calling her. "You're right. He hasn't answered it since he left last evening. My best guess is that he turned it off so no one could find him."

"But don't you have that *find my iPhone* thing?"

"He doesn't have an iPhone and the app just shows me where he was when his phone was turned off."

She huffs and I take a moment to just…breathe. Sheena's worried about her best friend, and she doesn't have a lover to fuck when she's feeling bad.

Or maybe she does and she's just discreet. I shouldn't make assumptions. At any rate, I give her time to get herself sorted.

"You have no idea where he is?"

I stifle a sigh. "That's why we called you. Figured you might have some idea where he'd go to hide out."

"I don't…hell. If I think of something I'll let you know."

"Thanks."

"Yeah, and I'm sorry if I was rude last night. Tell Connor I still think he's an asshole, though."

I give an exaggerated nod, even though she can't see me. "Will do. Call if you think of something." Useful, I almost add. Connor really shouldn't have called her a princess.

Sheena ends the call and the phone immediately buzzes with a text message. Lydia would be happy to share a beverage and could I meet her at eight?

Is it okay if Connor tags along?

Lydia doesn't have anything against Connor, as far as I know, but if she wants to meet at the ladies' bar, I should probably leave him home. Since I'm an honorary lesbian and all.

Sure. Be at the Tangle in an hour. It's a block or so away from the usual place on La Brea.

I text a confirmation and rap on the bathroom door. "Dude, we've got a date with a werewolf."

CHAPTER FOURTEEN

The first thing that greets me is the smell of wolf. Muscles rigid with tension, I lay still on the cave's floor and listen. The only thing disrupting the desert's evening song is the soft whuffing of a sleeper's breath.

Straightening, I ignore the stiffness in my joints and survey the space. There. There's a hump near the entrance that's a different color than the cave's floor. I stand on creaking knees and stumble over to the hump.

It's a wolf, curled up and snoring softly.

Not my wolf, however. My belly twists with disappointment. This one's a roan and its fur is matted and dirty.

I poke the beast with my toe and get a baleful glare for my trouble. "Am I in your way?" I ask.

The wolf bares its teeth. I bare mine. *Vampire. I win.* The wolf huffs, scrambling to its feet. In a flash of light and heat the creature shifts. I take a step back to avoid the sparks, muscles tense and my guard up.

The clerk from the motel stands buck naked in front of me. She's all muscle and sinew and uncombed hair. After a quick once-over, I stay locked on her eyes so I'll know if she's going to do anything shady.

It doesn't take long before she dodges my gaze. "Had a weird visitor last night after you left."

Chills run over my skin. "So?"

"He was this shady customer and he said he was looking for a vampire."

I try to imagine what this naked wolf person would consider shady and come up blank. "Did you get his name?"

"Said it was Winston Churchill and offered me $100 and his phone number, said I should text him if I met someone named Trajan Gall."

Fuck.

"He said you'd be big and dumb and Italian," she begins slowly. "I coulda just said, yeah, the dude you want is up the road a bit, hiding in a cave."

"But you didn't?"

"I didn't." She shakes his head as if she can't believe it herself. "Even when he flashed me a C-note, I didn't."

"Nice of you." I hope she can't see I'm twitching like a cat in a strange room. "Looks like I owe you one."

She scratches at her belly. "Maybe. Maybe not. I could still text the guy."

I bite back the first three things I want to say; *Not if you're dead* tops the list. "What'd this Winston Churchill look like?"

"Not tall. My height, or thereabouts. And kinda dreamy, you know, like one of those romantic poets my high school English teacher thought we should read. High cheekbones, permanent bedhead, a silk shirt that probably cost more than my rent."

"I imagine." She hasn't described David, which reassures me, but there are at least three of Jacques' scions who fit the romantic poet description, including Levy.

Jacques has a type, but he only discovered it after me.

"So you came up here and slept in the doorway to, what? Keep out anyone who might be looking for me?"

"No, sir, I stayed up here so I'd see you when you rose."

"Why?" I blink at her in confusion, and she stands naked with no self-consciousness at all.

"Because even though you're a vamp, you smell like pack, and I want to know why."

"I...what?" Shock puts a pause between the words, and since she raised the issue, I inhale deeply. She still smells like wolf, but only one wolf, not a bakers' dozen like this morning.

"Like pack. Like wolf pack. Who the hell are you?"

"Name's Trajan Gall. Who are you?"

"Heathercliffe Mountbatten." Her lips twist into something close to a grin. "Mom loved *Wuthering Heights* but I turned out to be a girl."

"Do you go by Heather or —"

"Cliffe. With an e."

"Why don't you put some clothes on, Cliffe with an e, and we can talk."

"Okay vampire Gall, see ya in a minute."

She pivots and heads for the cave's entrance. There's still enough light left to cast the smudge of a shadow on the cave floor. She grabs a bag from the pile of rocks and by the time she's dressed, the sun has set.

Her tee shirt has costume characters that I don't recognize and her Doc Martens' are unlaced and somehow that makes me feel old. "Come on," she says. "We can go over to Chuckie's. It won't be crowded this early."

"Chuckie's is a bar?"

"Restaurant. Sells pizza and Indian food."

"Do they have tequila?"

Her grin shines through the gloom. "I imagine they'll have something vampire-friendly."

Half-convinced this is a bad idea, I follow her. We retrace our route to the motel and go past it around the block.

Chuckie's turns out to be another low-profile building with white walls and a red roof, a look that seems to be a theme for the desert. If the hostess is put off by our unwashed appearance, she doesn't let it show. She points us to a table by the front window, but Cliffe asks for a table in the corner and she obliges.

The room is spacious, the walls divided by a chair rail molding, the bottom half painted saffron yellow and the top white. We sit across from each other—I grab the seat with my back to the wall so I can see the whole room—and manage to avoid any conversation at all while she pours our water.

Cliffe orders a beer and I ask for tequila. Again, the waitress doesn't miss a beat and heads off toward the bar. Either she's a little stoned or this place gets more than its share of weirdos.

Jacques' voice is a distant echo, easily ignored. The silence grows heavy by the time the waitress brings our drinks. I'm not sure I want to break it, but I raise my glass. "Here's to keeping secrets."

"I'll drink to that." Cliffe knocks her glass against mine. "Does that mean you're not going to tell me why you smell like a wolf pack?"

"I smell like your pack or just any wolf pack?"

"Any. My pack, well, that's another story."

One I'm not sure I want to hear. Swirling the tequila in my glass, I weigh how much to say. "I'm not sure I can explain."

"Try me."

I can't really see a reason not to give her a brief answer. "One of my boyfriends got cut out of his pack and more or less bonded with me and our third."

"More or less bonded? He can't just make his own pack. Is your third a wolf?"

"Nope." *And I'm* really *not going to get into any long stories about Connor.*

"You know that's not possible. What you just said. Wolves who get cut out of their pack die. They don't make themselves a new pack, and especially not with not-wolves."

"You asked. I told you." I shrug, hoping she'll leave it alone.

Yeah, like that's possible.

She's midway through a swallow of beer when she chokes. "Oh shit." She forces the words out between coughing spasms. "One of Alpha Collins' kids got cut out of his pack and then took down his uncle in *beurteilung*. You're in a pack with a Collins. That has to be it."

I push the hair out of my face, reluctant to say the words out loud.

"Fine. I'm right. Your poker face isn't all that. So tell me why you're here instead of with your pack?"

I look for answers in the bottom of my tequila shot. "It's complicated."

"Sure." She laughs. "Complicated like you pissed your boyfriend off or complicated like being a psychic lesbian werewolf living in the desert?"

"Neither, really, although you get points for honesty." I give her an appraising look. Under the dirt there's a young woman with good bone structure and an intelligent gaze.

And every IQ point in her gaze tells me to back the fuck off. "If you're in a pack with one of the Collins kids, you outrank me, and either way you could just whammy me."

"Whammy you?"

"Take over my brain and force me to tell you the truth."

I grin at my tequila. "Do I seem like the whammy-ing type?"

"Vampire, dude. It comes with the territory."

I use a long sip of tequila to give myself time to think. Having a psychic at hand might come in useful. "I did wonder about that thing you said yesterday."

"You'll have to tell me all about it. I never remember what my other sense says."

"Your other sense?"

"Yeah. That thing that makes me spout nonsense at odd moments, usually timed to totally embarrass me."

I need to learn more. "So you can't control it?"

"Nope." She leans back in her seat. "But working the night shift at the Shady Acres here limits the number of times I freak people out."

"And your pack..." I let the thought fade so she doesn't feel pressured.

"Imploded." She answers readily enough, so I give her an expectant nod.

She rolls her eyes like she's humoring me. "Our alpha died in a motorcycle accident and the rest of us sorta fragmented. Except none of the little pack-lets wanted to take on a lesbian psychic who has the habit of making weird announcements that might or might not be true."

My shot glass is empty, and I spin it on the table. "Too bad you can't perform on command. I could use a psychic right about now." I'm not sure how, but having one around seems like a good idea.

Her shoulders sag. "Yeah, well, this patch of earth suits me fine. I can run the desert when the moon is full and it's been a good six months since anyone told me I was crazy."

The bravado in her tone does a poor job of covering a larger hurt.

"Forget I said anything, then. An unconventional pack might well be your thing, but you're not stupid enough to get involved in my shitstorm right now."

She straightens, her gaze narrowing. "How bad is it?"

"Bad."

The waitress interrupts us and I send her off for another round. When she leaves, Cliffe stares into her beer. "I might be able to find you a permit so you can stay at the hotel."

"I don't know how long I'll be staying."

She glances at me. "Me neither."

"I'd appreciate the permit. We should talk again before I go." The words are out before my common sense can reel them back in. Her smile is tentative, like she's been disappointed too often to have much hope. I want to smack myself, but figure I'll save that for David when he finds out I've brought home a stray.

Assuming I go back. As much as I miss Connor and David, putting distance between me and Jacques was a good idea. It won't last forever, but I'll take it for now.

CHAPTER FIFTEEN

Connor in business mode is different than any other version. He stands straighter — if that's even possible — and he carries himself in a way that doesn't invite questions.

I mean, he'll never be a slouching surfer dude, but this is new.

Following him down a fluorescent-bright hallway, I do my best imitation of his walk. I might even be half an inch taller because of it. Well, maybe not, but a guy can dream.

We're at Headquarters for the Elites, where Connor has arranged to meet someone he described as a Sensitive. I'm just along for the ride on this one, and I promise myself I'll keep my mouth shut, or come as close to it as possible.

We enter a conference room with a large center table surrounded by leather padded chairs. One wall is windows, and a woman sits with her back to them. She's gazing into space, a blank piece of paper in front of her. She holds a pencil in her right hand, but she's not writing anything. Maybe she's waiting for the angels to speak or something.

"As far as I know," she says, her voice deeper than I expected, "those you call angels don't communicate in a way a mere human can understand. I get my best information from lesser beings."

I stop in the doorway, blushing to my bleached blond roots. "My mistake."

If Connor's curious about this little exchange, he doesn't let it show. He stops behind one of the seats, leaving space between himself and the woman. "Melinda Barwell?"

"You must be MacPherson, the one they call Mack."

"That's me." He extends his hand to shake. She grasps it, her eyes widening as if he's hotter than she expected.

"And this is my friend David," he says. I don't extend my hand. Meeting her gaze is awkward enough. At a glance, she's taken stock of my entire person, good and bad.

I pretty much wish I'd stayed in the car.

"Okay if we sit?" Connor asks, because she hasn't given us any indication that we're welcome to stay.

"I'd rather you didn't."

Her expression is as bland as oatmeal, but her tone makes both of us take a step back.

"We've never met before, Mack, but Poole has told me about you. I don't know who your young friend is, but the energy binding the two of you makes it hard for me to focus on anything else."

Jesus, maybe we shouldn't have had sex.

I edge toward the door and Melinda takes a long, slow breath. She's about forty, her curly brown hair sparked with silver. "Pose your question," she says, "and I will do my best to answer."

Connor steps forward just long enough to place a manilla envelope on the table. "We're looking for Princess Tatiana Ivanova. She's been missing for some four years, and we have reason to believe she's being held by the vampire Jacques Betancourt."

He pauses, giving her time to ask a question or make a comment, but Melinda's attention is fixed on the envelope. With a slight shrug, he continues. "We also suspect she's being held somewhere near the ocean, close enough to hear the waves."

That earns him a raised eyebrow. "That's a fairly specific detail. Any chance you'll tell me how you came up with it?"

We looked in a fake Harry Potter mirror. The thought's there before I can stop it and the

Sensitive pins me with a glare. "That doesn't seem like a credible source."

"We're not sure if it's credible or not." Connor steps forward, drawing her attention. "I've brought you some photos and a list of possible addresses. If you could look those over and let me know if anything pings for you—"

"It would be better to have one of her personal possessions."

Connor's expression doesn't change. "If I can find something of hers, I'll bring it to you. In the meantime, I'd appreciate it if you'd look through the stuff in the envelope."

He backs up a step and I'm already out the door. Sensitive Melinda has gone back to gazing at nothing. "I'll be in touch," she says, so faintly I wonder if I've imagined it. I take that as our cue to leave, so I do, Connor right behind me.

"I give you even odds that she'll come up with something," I say. The elevator chooses that moment to arrive and we climb aboard.

"Optimist," Connor says. The elevator doors close, and we descend to the main floor.

"Hopefully Lydia can come up with something more concrete."

"Hopefully."

By the time we get to La Brea, I've shaken off the weird woo-woo vibes the Sensitive left me with. Connor seems to get my mood, although he doesn't say anything. He keeps a hand on me, subtle touches that deliver comfort and possessiveness in equal measure.

The Tangle is a classic LA bistro, all hard edges and mood lighting. By the time we find Lydia, I've heard "my agent *blah*" and "my script *la la*" and "my new project *wah wah wah*" more than once. LA. It's an industry town.

Lydia's got a table in the corner. A younger and decidedly more femme woman sits next to her. Both of them are in black leather, but where Lydia looks like she's got nunchucks hanging from her belt, her friend's wearing a bustier and stiletto heels.

"This is Accalia," Lydia says, her arm draped along the back of her friend's chair.

I introduce myself and Connor and we join them at their table. A pretty waiter minces over, his glossy black hair a perfect architectural blunt cut. I order the fussiest thing on their menu, mainly because I'm jealous of his hair, and Connor orders a beer.

At least it's an IPA and not an uber-classy Budweiser.

We keep things safe and easy while we're waiting for our drinks, but still manage to establish some ground rules. Lydia and I are friends, Connor's keeping his mouth shut, and

Accalia might not be Lydia's consort yet, but she's well on her way.

Mazel tov.

My drink is frozen layers of red, blue, and yellow, and garnished with a bright orange sugared nasturtium. Or at least that's what the menu says. Connor mumbles something about a *fancy Slurpee* and takes a swallow of his beer. I ignore him and take a sip.

Okay, it tastes like a Slurpee with a kick, but whatever.

Accalia interrupts us with a well-timed throat clear. "I heard your name, you know."

She's looking at me but I glance at Lydia, who's busy staring at Accalia's profile.

"I hope it was a good thing." I try to laugh it off, but she pierces me with a blue-eyed stare.

"Maybe." Her smile is dry, cool. "I told Lyd I'd heard some cocky motherfucker had formed an unauthorized pack, and she said she knew who it had to be."

Connor's relaxed, beer in one hand, my knee in the other. I figure I don't know Lydia's sweetie well enough to make any grand proclamations, but a little fishing couldn't hurt.

"Unauthorized pack? Never knew there was such a thing."

Accalia's smile widens, showing too many teeth. "Huh. You look like you've lived in a city before, and places have rules, you know? Can't have just any group of dirtbags calling themselves a pack."

Lydia's gaze hasn't left her girlfriend's face, but right about the time I'm ready to start a smack-down because *hell yes I'm from a city*, she speaks up. "Yeah, so Cally, I told you David was likely the guy, but not so you could piss him off." She looks at me with an apologetic shrug. Between that and how bright pink Accalia's cheeks turn, I manage to deescalate.

"And this information is from a trustworthy source?" I mean, I know it's true, because I've got the summons from the LA Were Authority to prove it, but I'm curious about who she heard it from.

"I work for Tim Huggins," she says, all prim like I should be impressed by the name.

Lydia cuffs her shoulder, the alpha putting a lesser wolf in place. "He's the head of the LA Were Authority."

"So you know about the unauthorized pack because you saw the summons."

"I wrote it."

Connor chokes behind his hand, which makes it harder for me to stifle a laugh.

"Congratulations then," I say. "You spelled my name correctly."

She sits so straight I wonder who's shoved a ruler up her butt. Also, why the hell is Lydia involved with this nonsense? I mean, Accalia's pretty and all, but that doesn't make up for being nasty.

She's still aiming her next shot when I'm distracted by a trio of men, or more accurately, elves. They're headed in our direction, and I know that by the way Connor's hand freezes with his beer to his lips. His burst of tension has my wolf on alert.

"I'm looking forward to your testimony."

Or at least I think that's what Accalia says. My attention is locked on the lanky redhead with his left hand on his hip, casually holding his jacket open to show off the gun.

CHAPTER SIXTEEN

Spending one day in a cave had been necessary. Spending a second would be unnecessarily uncomfortable. Fortunately, Cliffe produces the correct permit so I have a room on the second floor of the High Desert Motel.

It isn't fancy, but it beats sleeping on the ground.

Still, I literally have nothing to do but sit in the room's only chair and wonder if I'll be up to the task of turning a human. It's easier than wondering if I'll truly be able to break from Jacques.

The television is playing whatever station the last guest watched. I'd left my laptop and my overnight bag with Connor and David. On my way out of town, I'd drawn as much cash as I could from a bank machine, and after Cliffe went to work, I'd done some shopping. Now I can keep myself clean and dressed, if not entertained.

Any vampire soon learns how to wait out the night. After all, when you know you'll never run out of time, there's less incentive to cram every waking moment with activity.

But tonight I can't find my equilibrium. Too many stressors compete for my attention. I finally give in and turn on my phone, which immediately erupts in a slew of voicemails, text messages, and emails.

I only listen to one voicemail. From Sheena.

"Trajan Gall, whatever is going on, you'd be better off with your friends around you. Even that asshole Connor has your back."

I debate returning her call. I debate sending a text. I do neither.

I shut my phone off and stare at the nubby grey carpet, hoping I haven't pinged off a satellite in a way that will lead anyone here.

Even Sheena.

Who isn't wrong.

I'm still at cross purposes with myself when Jacques arrives. He—or rather, his spirit—strolls though the hotel room door, his cold silver eyes the color of moonlight. He wears a hand-tailored suit and he's holding a handkerchief, as if he can't go long without coughing up blood. I don't move.

I can't. If he's found me here, I'm not safe anywhere.

"I thought vampires couldn't enter where they haven't been invited." I keep my voice level, hiding anger, disguising fear. At least this time I can talk.

He leans against the dresser. The pallor of his hands is nearly indistinguishable from the light pine. "I have a standing invitation."

Our gazes clash, hold. His expensive suit hangs on bony shoulders. A hard cough wracks him, stirring up something in me that feels like pity.

Almost.

"Well, you're here now. What do you want?"

"You're like a child in some kind of rebellious phase."

"That tells me how little you know about children."

Jacques' laugh is flinty. "Sarcasm is for the weak."

I don't react to his jibe. I've spent one hundred and fifty years planning every word I said to Jacques Betancourt, and a habit that long-lived won't fade easily.

The only easy thing is not to respond at all, yet I surprise myself.

"For fucks' sake, Jacques. You demanded that I kill my lover, and I will not." Anger flares, sending me up from the chair to face him. Shadows move through his form, confirming that he's not physically present. "For all these years, I've done what you've asked, but this goes too far."

His expression hardens. "Yes, and all those years ago, I did what you asked. Now you have no choice."

"Really?" I come close to a sneer. "Then tell me why I must do this."

He draws himself up as if attitude alone will make him taller than I am. "Because I demand it of you."

"Not good enough, my friend."

He does grow taller, his spirit spreading out into the room. "You will do this."

I fight the urge to cross my arms, fearing I'll look like the child in his accusation. "Go away, Jacques. You have my answer."

"You think I'd let a pansy like you defy me? I took you out of a slum and gave you something more to do than sucking men's cocks for your dinner. You might think you have the power to defeat me, but you'll regret the day you decided to try."

With that rather melodramatic pronouncement, he vanishes. Relief allows me to draw a single deep breath before memory squeezes my chest so hard I might never breathe again.

I've walled off those years, Mama and me drifting through town after town along the big muddy river. I collapse into the chair, overcome by the memories: the smell, the cold, the dirt. The desperation in Mama's eyes when she couldn't find decent work and had to resort to the indecent.

I wish I could say she always kept me safe, but she hadn't. She couldn't. The world back then was too hard. The things I'd done, the things *we'd* done, had been necessary to survive.

Only later, after Mama died and I'd crossed paths with Jacques, could I afford to feel shame. He'd taught me manners and polished my rough edges, allowing me a new perspective on the squalor that had surrounded me.

That shame could not outweigh my pride at having survived at all, the whole of it colored with sadness over Mama's death.

And regret. So much regret.

I hate those memories, yet I value them, too. The young man who'd outlasted the river towns still exists in the vampire I've become, and though I shut his memory away, his grit will carry me through.

Jacques meant to hurt me, to weaken me, but all he's done is make me mad. That anger acts like a splash of cold water, grounding me in the present. He'd proven his spirit could follow me, although he isn't continuously in my head the way he'd been in LA.

I pocket my phone and head for the manager's office.

Cliffe is there, carefully painting her fingernails black. Either the rank smell of wolf is gone or acetone can conquer anything.

"If I told you I had to leave now, would you come with me?" I ask, stepping right into the issue we'd flirted with earlier. Keeping her close increases the chances that I'd be around if her extra sense decided to share whether it meant Connor wouldn't really die, or whether the cryptic message was aimed at Jacques.

Her expression is somewhere between hope and hopeless. "Yup."

"It might be soon, and we might travel further east before we go to LA."

She caps her nail polish and sets the bottle aside. "I probably don't want to know the details."

"Probably not."

"Let me make a phone call."

She picks up a black plastic thing that looks like a 1960s movie version of a phone of the future. Meanwhile, a cell phone sits next to her elbow on the desk. I point to it and mouth, "Can I use that?"

Rolling her eyes, she slides it toward me. She's reached the person she called, and while they talk, I decide who I should call—Sheena, David, or Connor.

I settle on Sheena because hers is the only phone number I have memorized, since I've known her the longest. I could get the other numbers from my contact list, but I don't want to turn on my phone.

I dial and after a couple of rings, it goes to voicemail. At the beep, I start in. "It's me, and I don't want to tell you where I am. This is about Jacques, and for now, it's best if I stay away from LA. Tell David and Connor I'll be in touch as soon as I can. Stay safe and keep your wits about you."

I'm sure she'll do plenty of reading between those lines, but that's okay. I hand the phone back to Cliffe, who's ready and waiting. She palms the phone and flashes a smile.

Her smile is three quarters bravado, one quarter uncertainty. "I told my manager I might be dealing with a personal emergency soon."

"I hope we can approach things in an organized fashion, but..." I shrug. "If you notice anything unusual, if that guy comes back or you see anyone weirder than normal or anything that makes you uncomfortable, trust your gut and get out of here."

That little pronouncement kills her smile. "Should I be armed?"

I weigh the relative strength of an armed werewolf against a vampire. "Only if you're an excellent shot."

That brings her smile back. "I am."

With that, I leave her. I climb into the Range Rover, and for a moment I give in to weariness. Jacques isn't living in my head, but he can still get at me. I'm alone, with one partial ally and an unknown number of enemies. Sheena said I'd be better off with my friends around me, but I'm not sure. I might kill one of them.

What's the best path forward?

The sky is the kind of dark the city never sees, and the desert around me is silent. Oh, I'm sure there are the small sounds made by nocturnal creatures, but compared to LA, the quiet is a heavy thing. The absence of sound lets my head clear, and I come to a realization.

I'm hungry. Quickly, before I can go off on another tangent, I google "Joshua Tree Hospital" and learn that the Hi-Desert Medical Center is a couple miles down the highway in the direction of Twentynine Palms. Grasping that small bit of information, I put the car in gear and drive.

Persuading the front desk security guard to let me in takes very little effort and talking the blood bank clerk out of an expired unit or two takes even less. The blood is cold and rank, nothing like the sweet sustenance I get from David and Connor, but I feel better after I drain the bags.

I'm in the hospital parking lot, taking stock. I'd left LA in a rush because I couldn't stand Jacques' voice in my head. Being here had solved that. Partially.

But I'm a couple hours away from anyone who truly has my back. Was my self-control really so weak?

Possibly?

I can't risk Jacques finding me. It's just after midnight, so I have time to get someplace safe. The only question is, should I go back to LA or go further away? And if I go back to LA, do I contact Delia Packard and make good on my promise? She's got my blood on her palm to force the issue if necessary.

I reach for the starter before I've made up my mind. I could take off now, leaving my few purchases for the hotel room's next occupant, but I did promise to pick up a psychic werewolf. Dragging someone new into this drama feels bad. Real bad. But so does leaving her behind.

A flash of movement catches my peripheral vision. Something or someone cast a shadow in the glare of the overhead light, so quick only a vampire could have seen it.

So quick only a vampire could have made it.

Ducking low, I ease open the Range Rover's door. Listen. Nothing. No sound, no movement. All this drama might be making me unusually jumpy, but I know what I saw. Common sense would have me put the car in gear and get the hell away. Instead, I slide to the ground and crouch low, leaving the door ajar.

There's a blur of motion to my left. An undead fucker stands motionless under the light. She's petite, her hair worn long and loose and her skin surprisingly tan.

A short, piercing whistle sounds from my right. There must be two of them. I hide in the SUV's shadow for another moment, then stand. There's three of them, not two, and none of them look familiar. That should be reassuring — at least Jacques hasn't sent his other children after me — but their vibe is pretty damned far from friendly.

"Is there a problem?" I ask, although their collective frowns make the answer evident.

"Yeah," the young one on my right says. He's dressed the way this generation thinks punk rockers did in the '80s, right down to the mohawk and safety pins in his ears. "You're trespassing."

Christ. I should have driven away. They're closing in, one step at a time. "I suppose it's too late for me to apologize."

"Yup," the girl says. She darts in and zaps me with a Taser before I can react.

Fuck me running, as David would say. That hurts. My knees give way and both arms flail. My only consolation is that I swat her good on the way down.

"What the fuck was that for?"

No one answers me, the bastards. The girl with the taser's sitting on her butt in the dirt so I'm safe from that for now, but the punk's coming at me with a zip tie in his hand.

Instead of waiting to see what they'll do next, I scramble to my feet. Guess when you've been a vampire as long as I have, a taser shot is like a bee sting, more annoying than anything else.

From the way his eyes pop, I wasn't supposed to be able to stand up so soon. Surprise stops his forward progress, anyway, which gives me time to argue some more.

"Look, kids, I'm sorry I drank your blood bank hand-out. I'll be going now, and we can stay friends."

The three baby vamps exchange glances, but it's the punk who speaks up. "As if."

As if? I shrug. "So we're not friends. I'm still leaving."

"You don't look like the kind of guy who has many friends." The third Musketeer laughs loud enough to make me wonder if he's playing with the same deck as the rest of us.

They can't be *that* isolated. Surely they've run across vamps who are older than they are. For all their overconfidence, none of them look like they can take me in a fight and I'm about out of patience. "Go back to your nursery school before one of you gets hurt."

"Fuck you," the punk says, giving me his best Billy Idol sneer.

"Seriously?" I cover the ground separating us faster than he can think. "I've got tee shirts older than you are, dumbass." I get a firm grip on one shoulder and spin him around so his back is to me. He starts thrashing so I pin his arms and lift him off the ground. He manages to tag my shin with the heel of his shitkicker boots and I slam him into the pavement. He bounces up, ready to come at me but I catch his gaze and hold it.

It's rude to mess with another vampire's mind. In fact, unless they're real young it's pretty much impossible. "Sit down, please." He does, the veins on his neck standing out from trying to fight me.

Maybe this'll teach him a lesson in manners.

I ease back a step, aiming in the direction of my SUV. The thud of footsteps draws my glance. The girl with the taser is coming in at a run so I take a quick step out of her way.

She runs past, and whatever she's hollering sure sounds angry.

"What about you?" I glance at the crazy one. "You want to give me a try?"

He just laughs, so he's not completely crazy.

Miss Taser's coming at me full speed again. I side-step her again and she shouts an obscenity, something to do with my parentage.

Before I can protest, she pivots and comes running, but this time I stop her with an outstretched hand. "You are wasting my time." I grip her upper arm and give her a shake. She's squirming and hollering and she pulls out a fancy little snub-nose pistol and puts a bullet in my biceps.

"Son of a bitch." I fling her into her punk rock friend. The bullet's not silver — these kids must be *really* young — but it still burns.

"On the count of three," the punk rocker says, but I don't wait around to see whatever foolishness they've come up with. I jump high enough to land on the roof of the Range Rover, coming to rest just in time for something to explode in the place I'd been standing.

Connor and David are going to crack the fuck up when I tell them this story. I'm laughing already, although my laughter might have a hysterical edge. I mean, how am I supposed to summon the strength to destroy my maker if three baby vamps can chase me onto the roof of my car?

They're huddling, clearly planning their next play. I have no weapons on me, nothing but fists and a bad attitude. Real quick I need to decide if I'm the just businessman, the guy who runs The Club, or if I'm something more. Because playing by the rules isn't going to help me.

"I'm done here," I mutter, and when Miss Taser gives a particularly shrill giggle, I leap.

My fangs out, I land roaring at their feet. The crazy one is smarter than he looks because he spins around and takes off running. I need to make a statement, one they won't misunderstand. I reach for the punk, stiffen my fingers, and hit him hard in the center of his chest.

With a quick flip of my wrist, I wrap my hand around his heart.

He freezes, arms outstretched, mouth working but no sound coming out. His dark blood wells up around my hand. The girl goes full wildcat, scratching and clawing, but I knock her aside. She must catch the look on his face because she latches on to my other arm.

"Stop. Oh my god Trevor, he's...stop. Don't hurt him." She shrieks so loud I wish I'd picked her heart instead. I grab her upper arm and shake her to make her shut up.

"Both of you listen before I see how far I can pitch this ball."

"You've got my full attention, man." The punk's voice is a bare rasp.

The girl doesn't answer, but she does quiet down.

"Okay, I apologized for visiting your blood bank. Are you going to let me go about my business, or do I have to give you a more extreme lesson in what can happen when you mess with a strange vampire?"

"You're killing him," the girl says between sobs. Pink tears outlined in black mascara streak her cheeks. "Stop. Please."

I let go of the punk's heart and wipe the blood off on his shirt. His body starts to knit itself together before I get my hand clean. Smiling to show off my fangs, I head for my Range Rover, keeping an eye on them over my shoulder. "See ya 'round."

Leftover vampire blood makes my hand stick to the steering wheel. I hear a clink, metal against glass. The chick's bullet pops out of my biceps with enough force to hit the window. I pull out of the parking lot, the baby vamps watching me go.

If I were human, my heart would be pounding and I'd be breathing hard.

I'm doing neither of those things.

Making a break from Jacques had always been my goal, but this little trip to the desert gave me time to think and reminded me I'm not human. I'm a vampire, and I'm done with people giving me grief.

Like you, Jacques. I'm coming for you.

CHAPTER SEVENTEEN

CONNOR

Kowalski." I greet the man civilly, despite the threat sparking off his bronze aura.

His answering grin lacks even a hint of warmth. "MacPherson."

David doesn't say anything, but he's radiating an appropriate amount of tension, given a guy with a gun just walked up to us.

"You wanted to talk to us."

"No, I want you to come with me. Now."

David growls, low, and both Lydia and her friend shift forward, alert and ready.

"I can tell you right here that I don't know where the Princess is, so—"

"And I can tell you right here that you're lying." Kowalski's voice rises above the clubby chatter in the room. The two guys he's with show off their weapons, ready for a fight. *Shit.*

If I can't talk these guys down, the wolves will follow me outside. Gang warfare, supernatural style. "All right. Let's try this again." I speak low and fast. "A couple nights ago, I visited the home of the Viscount Baltinglass. He keeps a mirror that shows you what you want most, and in it, I saw the Princess Tatiana. All she could tell me is that she can hear the ocean. The next night, a friend and I visited several houses that are owned by Jacques Betancourt. We think we found where he's staying, but it's nowhere near the ocean, so I don't think the Princess is there."

Kowalski's expression doesn't change, but his friends share a glance. Worried? Maybe. At any rate, it's a chink in their armor.

"Why didn't you come to me with this information?" Kowalski's found something new to be pissed off about. Not sure if that's a good thing, or…

"What information?" I half rise from my seat, hands on the table where they can be seen. "Should I have told you to search every beach in Southern California? I don't have anything more specific than that."

A muscle twitches in Kowalski's jaw. "What about the house where Betancourt is hiding? We could search there and—"

"And let him know we're getting close and he needs to move the Princess someplace new?" Kowalski's two friends definitely look worried, so I keep going. "Look, I came to you and said I wanted to find the Princess when no one else would. There's no rational reason for me to keep anything important from you."

"I don't believe you."

"*Dia á sábháil.* Why would I lie?" And why would the Princess herself imply Kowalski is the problem? That makes me even less likely to say anything.

"So you can give the Princess to your Morrigan."

David snickers and I clench my fists so I won't smack him. "There is no possible circumstance in which I'd give the Princess to Ananda Pendragon." *Unless she outright asks me to.* "I don't know who you've been talking to, but that won't happen."

"Enough." Kowalski speaks through gritted teeth. "Come outside now."

"If I go outside with you, my friends will follow."

"Then my friends will kill them."

David laughs out loud. "Come on, sugar britches. Try."

The waiter chooses this moment to arrive. He's a pretty thing, and David's doing a shit job of pretending to ignore the guy's perfect hair. The waiter leans over our table to pick up our empty glasses and looks me straight in the eye. "Can I get y'all another round? And by the way, the management will be incredibly unhappy if you provoke those assholes while they're in our establishment."

"So you're saying I should go outside with three armed elves?"

He pats my hand. "I'm sure you'll figure something out."

Gritting my teeth, I turn to Kowalski. He's relaxed a micrometer and one of his friends has his arms crossed, clearly giving up.

"I think you should pull up some chairs and let me buy you a drink." I've literally got my fingers crossed, hoping this defuses him. "I will tell you, in as much detail as possible, what my next steps will be."

"You're lying," Kowalski says, reaching for his gun.

"Jesus Christ, give it a rest, my dude." Accalia stands up, and although she's probably all of five foot one, she commands all of our attention. Kowalski does, in fact, let go of his gun. Color me impressed.

Accalia reaches into her little black clutch purse and pulls out a white business card. "See this? It says I'm a certified empath, and while I have very good shields, having three assholes, sorry, elves walk up with guns drawn disrupted my control."

Kowalski looks from the card to her face and back again. Whatever he sees must be convincing, because his shoulders slump.

"I can tell you with absolute certainty that Connor is telling you the whole truth as he knows it. There was no trace of a lie in his voice or in his words."

Now all three elves are looking uncomfortable. The waiter is still hovering, as if the soap opera playing out at our table is more entertaining that whatever's happening in the rest of his section. I catch his eye. "Can you help them find chairs and then bring them a round of whatever they want? I'm buying."

That breaks through their immobility and for a good three minutes there's a flurry of activity. Our table's not really big enough for seven, but we all crowd around, waiting for our drinks. I order coffee because I can't afford to be sloppy.

I wait until we're all settled to speak. "I'm not sure whether I'm more upset that you think I'd lie to you or angry that someone's out there spreading rumors."

"More than one someone," one of Kowalski's friends says. He's fair skinned with straw-colored blond hair. "I had at least three people tell me you'd found the Princess and were keeping her from us."

Between his earnest blue aura and his concerned smile, he's so sincere I almost believe him. Almost, but not quite. "What's your name?"

"Mikael."

"Did either of you two hear these rumors?" I point at Kowalski and his remaining friend.

"Not directly," Kowalski says, his expression guarded. "Did you, Ivan?"

The third elf is having trouble holding onto his glamour. His ears are way more pointed than any human's would be, and his eyes are a disturbing Kelly green. "Only from Mikael."

I turn my attention to Mikael, but he's locked in a staredown with David.

"Enough." I snap my fingers and they both jump. "Now tell me who you really heard these rumors from."

Mikael's earnestness has been replaced by a sardonic sneer. "Who *didn't* I hear them from? It's all over the place. You're a dead man and you're planning to take the Princess with you."

His accusation hits me like a punch to the gut. "What? That's not true."

Accalia and Lydia are having a wordless conversation. Finally the empath turns to me. "He's telling the truth, too."

"But I'm not dying and the only thing I want for the Princess is to return her to her family."

"Interesting. They're both telling the truth." Accalia settles back in her seat with a small frown.

"So here's what I think," Lydia says, and we all give her our attention. "I think you three"—she points at the elves—"are being fed bullshit from somewhere."

Accalia yelps, like she's going to interrupt, and Lydia takes hold of her hand. "Yeah, shug, I know you heard truth, but there must be a screwup somewhere. I also know"—she looks hard at the elves—"that Connor MacPherson can turn into a bodach, so unless you want to meet a specter of death, I'd suggest you back the hell off."

Kowalski gives me a measured look. "We're low on patience, MacPherson. Find the Princess and return her to us, or next time we won't bow to the whims of society."

The waiter sets a drink in front of him with a little smirk. "Yeah, you get extra credit for behaving in public. I know that's hard for an elf."

He spins away, his laughter trailing behind. David's laughing too, and Lydia's grinning broadly. Kowalski's staring at his drink like the waiter spit in it, a reasonable concern. For me, I'm ready for this night to be over. I can't remember why we came here in the first place, and as the conversation drags on around me, I get frustrated.

This isn't helping us get Trajan back. This isn't helping anything.

The elves finish their drinks and with a final barrage of warnings and threats, they leave. I'm ready to close out the tab, but David covers my credit card hand with his. "Hang on. Sheena'll be here in a minute."

I stifle a groan. "What does she want?"

"She says she talked with Trajan."

That's about the only response that could have kept me in my seat. The waiter refills my coffee and sure enough, Sheena comes through the door before I can add any cream.

Sheena's an imposing figure, no matter what she's wearing, but tonight she's channeling her inner Trinity. She's wearing shades and a black leather coat with exaggerated lapels and a wide belt. Her hair's in a tight bun, highlighting her elegant bone structure and her fierce frown.

We all stand and shake hands like grown-ups, and if Lydia keeps a hand on Accalia I can't blame her. Once we're seated, David flags the waiter and Sheena shrugs out of her coat.

"David says you heard from Trajan," I say, leaving space for her to answer the question I haven't quite asked.

She nods, and while she doesn't look happy, I don't get the sense that I'm the object of her ire. "He must have borrowed a phone, and of course he called when I was in the shower. He left a voicemail saying he needed to stay out of LA but to tell you two that he was okay and he'd be in touch soon." She frowns in the direction of the frilly drink David's got in front of him. It's his third, but he'll be fine. Werewolf.

"He said to keep my wits about me" — she smiles, propped on her elbows, like we're besties having a little gab session — "and now you need to tell me what the hell is really going on."

"Got my curiosity too," Lydia says, and I realize she and Accalia are going to hear more than we might want them to. I'm still pondering the implications of that when David starts to talk.

"A while ago Trajan's maker commanded him to kill Connor, and we're trying to figure out an alternative solution."

Sheena nods like that's not new information, and Lydia takes the straw from her drink and bends it in half, her attention locked on David. "Such as?"

David's expression goes stern. "Trajan needs to break from Jacques."

"I assume these are vampires." Accalia glances from David to Lydia and back.

"Yeah." Lydia shoots her a smile, all the while twisting the straw in a tight spiral. "You're going to have to kill him. Jacques, I mean."

"Yup." I drop the word into the middle of us and and it lies there quivering.

"Why?"

"I think it's tied up with the missing elven princess." *I think*, nothing. I'm pretty damned sure that's the connection.

"We think we know where Jacques is staying," David says, "but if you hear anything that might be helpful…"

"I've heard something." Sheena's expression turns somber. "Betancourt's calling in all his favors. From what I hear, anyone who's even thought about asking him for something is expected to be ready."

"Dang, that's not good." David smacks the tabletop. "What the hell is he up to?"

"He's going to build a giant fire." Ananda Pendragon, the Morrigan, spins one of the empty chairs at our table and drops into it. "And he's going to burn what's left of Princess Tatiana." She scowls around the table. "And then he's going to trap her spirit in a magic web, so he can drain her life force and use it to extend his own."

"His own life?" Accalia's the only one who doesn't seem intimidated by my great-whatever grandmother.

"Yes." The Morrigan gives her a speculative look. "Jacques Betancourt is dying."

"How do you know?" David's tone is genial but his expression radiates suspicion.

Ananda Pendragon's smile is pure evil. "I made a friend. Come here, friend."

A man stumbles over. A man, or a phouka. His features are familiar, and not just because all phoukas look alike.

"We've met before." I wrack my brain for the answer.

"Yeah. You snuck into Mr. Betancourt's house and I caught you. I'm Dash Dolivo and if you don't stop Mr. Betancourt, we're all gonna die."

CHAPTER EIGHTEEN

Trajan

Cliffe's eyes get wide when I stalk into the motel office. "That was awful fast to have you looking so disturbed."

I come to a stop in front of her desk. "I didn't have to go far."

"Why?"

"I stopped at the hospital to see a man about some blood and ran into a trio of baby vampires. They thought they could take me and I came close to tearing the heart out of some kid who looked like an extra from *The Lost Boys*."

I don't waste time watching many vampire films, but Kiefer Sutherland's a classic.

"Probably Trevor." She caught her lower lip in her teeth. "I can see where he'd make you want to damage him. He's annoying a-f."

"He and his friends gave me the distinct impression they'd never met a vampire who was more than twenty years old."

Her eyes widened further. "How old are you?"

I raise one eyebrow. "If you have to ask…"

"Hoo-kay."

Still not sure why I came back, I try for an angle that'll make sense to myself as well as a relative stranger. "An hour ago when I asked if you'd come with me, you said yes, but before we do this, you need to know a little bit more about what you'll be walking into. My maker commanded me to kill my lover. I said no. Now my maker has a direct line inside my head and he's threatening to kill me. Putting distance between us helped shut him up but tangling with your annoying vampire friend proves that assholes are everywhere and what I really need to do is go back to LA and face Jacques myself."

She blinks once. Twice. "You should have had me take notes."

"I'm betting you remember enough." I snort a laugh. "Anyway, the taxi's leaving. You don't have to come with me now. We can exchange contact information and if you get a sudden urge to meet up with an unusual pack—assuming we survive—we'd be happy to host you for dinner or something. I don't mean to discourage you, but it's quite likely I'm walking into a fight of supernatural proportions."

She glances around the office as if taking a snapshot for posterity. "Let me make a call."

While I wait, I turn my cell phone on. I'm done hiding. I'm also crazy for bringing a stranger into the midst of this. David's going to freak out. I squash that thought and swipe the screen.

My first call is to Delia Packard. She doesn't answer—I don't expect her to—so I leave a polite voicemail letting her know I'm ready. Next, I text David and Connor.

On my way home. I'll text you when I get closer.

I send David a separate text.

Bringing someone who might want to join the pack.

Because yeah, the only way out of this mess is through.

CHAPTER NINETEEN

ash fucking Dolivo. What kind of name is that? Seriously. He's classic phouka: dark curls, green eyes, and a cleft chin. His half-smile isn't too far from a dog's sloppy grin. He must be Betancourt's…what? Court jester?

"Explain." Connor's one-word command makes me twitch in my seat. He's got his game face on, the one he must have worn as an Elite, a side of him I've only seen once or twice.

Dolivo squirms, too. "Mr. Betancourt has been getting deliveries of all kinds of stuff. Black magic stuff."

"Any idea what he's going to do with it?"

Dolivo opens his mouth, pauses to chew on his lower lip, then brightens. "I—"

"He doesn't know." The dark-haired woman makes a slicing motion with her hand. "I've questioned him at length. It's enough to know that Jacques Betancourt has the Princess Tatiana and is planning something diabolical."

"Diabolical?" Connor's tone is measured, and I cover my mouth to hide the laugh that I can't stifle. Melodrama much?

The woman—we haven't been introduced but Connor clearly knows who she is—reeks of power and her attitude toward Dash Dolivo is one of tolerance. I think about introducing myself, but Connor's still looking fierce, so I decide anonymity is better.

"Have either of you heard of Clapton Industries?" Connor poses the question to the new arrivals, but it's Accalia who responds first.

"They deal in magical materials." She takes out her phone and swipes the screen. "The Were Authority has been monitoring them because there have been reports that some of their shipments are less than legal."

Dash nods, as if he's heard that before. "I bet half of the boxes that have been delivered to Mr. Betancourt's house have Clapton Industries on their mailing labels."

"Wait, you know where Betancourt is hiding?" I pipe up, even though this is really Connor's territory.

"He's not hiding." Dash gives me his happy puppy smile. "We had an accident at his other house, so we're—"

"In the house in the hills over Santa Monica?" Connor asks.

The puppy grin slips. "Well, yeah, but no one's supposed to know that."

I catch Lydia's eye. The angle of her brow says she and Accalia are ready to move along, and I can't blame them. Still, Connor's in detective mode so I try not to fidget. If he can get something meaningful out of the phouka, it'll help Trajan.

Hell, if Connor gets something meaningful out of this flake, I'll never call him Pookie again.

Maybe.

"But that's not where he's keeping the Princess, is it." The pitch of Connor's voice drops. He's made a statement, not asked a question.

The woman who brought Dash to us tenses, her glare so hot I wonder how Connor doesn't wilt. The phouka doesn't say anything, even when she pokes him.

"He won't tell me," she snaps.

"I can't." It's Dash's voice, but the words are forced between clenched teeth.

The woman gives a disgusted huff and points at Connor. "Find her or I'm going to make you regret it."

Connor slides back in his seat, his hands spread on the tabletop. "Of course, *onóir amháin.* I live to serve."

Okay, he had me until the sarcasm. I'm coiled, ready to spring under the table if the woman starts shooting fire out of her fingertips. There's not a doubt in my mind that she could.

"*Meascach.*" The growl in her voice makes the hair on my neck stand up straight.

Connor just sits there, head cocked like he's daring her to take a shot. The tension grows so thick even Lydia starts to look worried, a single crease forming between her brows. Accalia must have ice in her veins because she's still fussing with her phone like we're debating our next round of cocktails.

The woman blinks first. "Enough." She springs out of her seat, dragging Dash with her. "I want word from you. Soon."

Making a diva turn, she strides toward the door. The phouka waves over his shoulder, his expression somewhere between worry and terror. "Too bad you didn't get a crack at him without his keeper," I murmur, and Connor chuckles.

"Not sure it would have done me much good. He's got some kind of hex that's keeping him from answering that specific question. She'll kill him before she gets anything out of him."

"Huh. Now I feel bad that we didn't keep him here."

Connor's expression grows thoughtful. "Yeah."

"Ordinarily I'd complain that you didn't introduce us to whoever that was," Accalia says. "She could give me nightmares."

"Ananda Pendragon, the Morrigan."

I jump and Accalia yelps, "No way." Even Lydia laughs.

"Yes, that was the living god and my many-times great grandmother. I sincerely hope none of you run across her again."

"Elves, goddesses; is there anybody you haven't pissed off," Lydia murmurs.

Connor catches my eye and laughs. "Give me time," he says, and I shake my head.

We order another round because nerves, and during our conversation I manage to point out that the Were Authority hearing on my unauthorized pack formation was poorly timed.

"It'll be fine, David," Lydia says, giving Accalia a hard look. "It's just a formality."

Accalia doesn't say anything and while I should be reassured, I'm not. They take off soon after that, with a final warning regarding Jacques.

"He's winding things up, I hear," Lydia says. "Pulling together allies so when it's time for whatever he's planning, he'll have plenty of help."

Neat.

I'm disappointed when a waitress picks up my debit card, instead of the waiter with the perfect hair. *Oh well.* We've got time to kill and I still have questions. "So is your great-whatever grandmother on your mother's side or your father's?"

"Mother's." Connor's dry tone suggests that further questions will be unwelcome—so of course I keep going.

"Who's your father?"

The silence between us drags on long enough that I'm reframing the question when he finally answers. "I don't know, David. My mother would never tell me, so I learned not to ask."

There's a warning in his voice, as if I should learn not to ask, too. "But he must be a supernatural being of some kind. I mean, a bodach isn't a Tuatha Dé Danann trait."

"I know," he says tightly.

"Aren't you curious?"

He doesn't answer, but the way the muscles in his jaw work tell me I've pushed hard enough for one night. "Well, whoever he is, he must be powerful a-f, because I'm pretty sure you just told a living god to go to hell." I speak lightly and he relaxes a skosh.

Our phones chime at the same time. I get to mine first. "Hey, it's Trajan."

Headed back. Where can I find you?

I'm bringing someone who might want to join the pack.

Connor stares at his phone, one hand massaging the back of his neck. I can't read his expression, but if he's feeling ambivalent, I can't blame him. I ignore the bit about bringing a new pack member. *WTF, Guido?*

"Where should we tell him to meet us?" I keep my voice calm to give Connor the space he might need.

He straightens, chin raised as if he's ready to take a punch. "Tell him where we're staying and ask him what time he'll be there."

I inhale slowly, let it go, then send the text. My lovers are brave, both of them. Time for me to ball up, too.

PART THREE: NO MURDER. NO HOW.

CHAPTER TWENTY

TRAJAN

Motel 6? Clearly David wasn't involved in booking this place. I park the Range Rover, staring up at the building. Eight stories high, sixteen rooms wide, it's a bulky block that glows gold where the rooms are lit from within.

"Tell me again why we're here?" Cliffe plays with one of the leather thongs wrapped around her wrist, twisting it tight and letting it go. Her nerves are a faint echo of my own.

Jacques has been in my head since we passed San Bernardino, a constant refrain of *kill, obey, kill.* "My boyfriends are staying here."

She mouths an echo of my statement, and even though it's only one in the morning, I'm tired. I'm no longer worried I'll act on Jacques' command, but his barrage of bullshit is draining.

I just hope nothing changes when Connor is standing in front of me.

"Let's go." I pop the locks. Cliffe follows me out of the SUV and into the brightly lit hotel lobby. She's got a duffel bag slung over one shoulder and although her expression is bland, I sense her rapid heartbeat.

The wait for the elevator lasts forever. We take it to the sixth floor and reach their hotel-room door in about four heartbeats.

The door opens before I knock. David's there. His nostrils flare, as if surprised to see me.

Or surprised to see Cliffe.

I reach for him, and he folds himself into my arms. "Hey, puppy." My voice cracks and I shut up.

We hold each other until Connor pulls the door wide. "*Mo shíorghrá.*"

"*Amore mio.*" Clasping Connor's hand, I keep David tucked under my chin. "I went to the desert where the air was clear. It helped me think."

"I'm glad." He squeezes my hand, his gaze drifting over to Cliffe. "Who's the new recruit?"

"I'm Heathercliffe Mountbatten." Her tone is confident, but her eyes are scared. "But call me Cliffe with an e."

I clear my throat. "I realize the timing is bad, but…"

Laughing, David knocks the side of his fists against my ribs. "Bad? You think the timing is only bad?" He steps away from me and offers Cliffe his hand. "Welcome to chaos central. I'm not sure how to pronounce Cliffe with an e, and I hope you like a good fight."

"I do," she says, and they shake on it.

"You're not a lone wolf." David doesn't let go of her hand. "Are you looking for a pack?"

She meets him head on. "No, or at least I wasn't."

"Cliffe has other skills," I say, ignoring her raised eyebrow.

"Which skill?" she snaps. "The lesbian one or the psychic one?"

David lets her hand slide out of his. "You might be better off with Lydia. All her girls swing that way, and they're not currently in the middle of a murderous vampire row."

"Whatever you say."

Connor puts a hand on David's shoulder. "Let's take this out of the hallway, anyway."

We sidle into the room. It's barely bigger than the two queen-sized beds and, weirdly, one wall is painted orange. There's nothing soft or warm or welcoming about the place, but then I haven't been overcome by the urge to damage Connor, so I'll take what I can get.

There's only one chair in the room and I wave Cliffe into it. David and Connor sit on one of the beds, and I remain standing. My nerves are jangling. I figure I've got twenty-five words to make this right.

"Cliffe helped me out." Talking is easier if I look at the floor. "And I figure we need allies right now."

"The more the merrier?"

I slide a glance at David. His brows are drawn, but like he's puzzled rather than angry.

"Though you make a good point about Lydia," I add.

Cliffe's so tense I'm afraid she might shatter and I'm pondering where to go next when Connor speaks up.

"Let's table this. You're welcome to hang with us for now, Cliffe, and once we get things settled, we'll come up with a solution that works for everyone."

She inhales, her smile shy. "That's fair."

Connor and David exchange glances. "Meanwhile," Connor says, "we have some new information."

He goes on to recap what they learned from Lydia and the Morrigan, about a magical bonfire, rumors and lies, and some guy named Dash Dolivo. They're just winding down when someone knocks on the door.

David and Connor both tense, but I wave them off. "It's Sheena. I texted her from the road."

"Why not take an ad in the LA Times," David murmurs, but I ignore him.

I let my oldest friend in and the first thing she does is slap me. Hard.

"Don't you ever go on walkabout without saying goodbye again." Still scowling, she wraps me in a hug.

"I'm sorry." I whisper the words in her ear and she pulls a handful of my hair.

"You better be."

I let her go and she immediately grabs my wrist. "Who's that?" She's pointing at Cliffe.

I make introductions but I leave out the part where Cliffe might join our pack. Now that I'm here, in the same room as David and Connor, I'm wondering if I made a mistake bringing Cliffe along.

"It's not like you to pick up strays," Sheena says. Cliffe's expression doesn't change, although she had to have heard.

"Leave it." David gives Sheena a stern look, which shuts her up but also makes her eyebrows rise.

"I'm glad you're here, Sheena," Connor says. "We need to plan our next steps."

I'm too antsy to stand still. "I left Delia Packard a voicemail. She should be getting back to me soon."

"Why?" Connor asks at the same time as David says, "Bad idea, Guido."

I glare at them both. "According to Delia, if I turn a human, I'll be better able to fight Jacques when I need to."

David's fiddling with his hair like it's going to change the subject for us and Sheena's eyes are narrowed.

"Turn a human into what?" Connor speaks slowly, as if he can guess the answer and doesn't like it.

"Into a vampire," I say simply. "One of her scions wants her lover to join her in her undeath, and I said I would do it."

Connor's on his feet and about eight inches from me before I can react. "No fucking way, Trajan. You'd be agreeing to take responsibility forever."

I speak to him, because he's *thisclose*, but I'm really addressing all of them. "Delia will monitor the new vampire, as he will become part of her household."

"Why doesn't she turn him?" Sheena asks from somewhere outside the bubble Connor has created.

"Because two scions of the same master don't always get along."

"You cannot do this thing." Connor puts a hand on my arm, his expression imploring me to stand down.

"Why not?"

"To bring someone else into the life you lead…" Connor's voice fades.

Or maybe my rising anger drowns out his words. "What's wrong with the life that I lead? I happen to enjoy it a great deal."

"No, you're fine. There's nothing wrong with you. I just…" Connor glances at David, who's got his hands clasped on top of his head, eyes wide like he can't believe what he's hearing.

My cell phone chooses that moment to chime. It's a text from an unknown number.

Madame Packard looks forward to seeing you at three minutes to midnight tonight.

"Too late." I pocket my phone, my guts twisting on themselves. "My mind's made up. I will do anything in my power to rid myself of

Jacques Betancourt. I hope you'll support me, but either way…" I shrug. It would be a painful irony if ridding myself of Jacques loses me Connor as well.

The silence between us reaches an uncomfortable point when Cliffe says, "I'll go with you."

"What?" I shoot her a glance.

"When you go this evening. You shouldn't go alone into a strange vampire's home, so I'll go too."

Her simple common sense wakes the rest of them.

"She's right. I'm in." Sheena sounds unconvinced, but I appreciate her support.

David rises from the bed and comes to stand between me and Connor. "Me too, although I understand where Connor's coming from."

"I will not, *mo shíorghrá*. There must be another way."

He's close enough I catch his leather and whiskey scent. I close my eyes. Jacques' voice grows stronger, though I no longer feel the need to give in. Connor moves away, taking his warmth and his scent with him.

I don't move. "When David decided to call *beurteilung* on his uncle, you supported him despite the substantial risk involved. When you defeated Adam Smith by turning yourself into a shadow of death, I did not remove myself from you. Why deny me your support now?"

I open my eyes. Connor's face is a mask of anguish and his words — *bring someone else into the life you lead* — run through my mind in Jacques' voice. There's nothing wrong with my life. Nothing.

"I am a vampire, *amore mio*. I have been one all these long years, and I see no shame in creating another such as myself. I'm sorry, but I must do this."

"I'm sorry too." Connor reaches for my hand and intertwines our fingers. "I'm going out for a while, but I'll be back before dawn."

With that, he leaves before anyone can react. David moves first, flinging the door open and hollering, "Get back here, you dumbass."

No response. He leans against the door jamb, hands covering his face. Sheena puts an arm around my shoulders and I lean into her strength.

From her chair in the corner, Cliffe chuckles. "You weren't fucking kidding, vampire Gall. You said there'd be fireworks, but dang."

"Did you just call him vampire Gall? Like, is that your nickname for him?" David peers at her from between his fingers.

"Apparently," I say, and David laughs. He crosses the room and rises on his toes to brush a kiss on my cheek.

"Give him a minute, Tony. He'll pull his head out of his ass and be back with an apology before we get around to missing him."

I pull David close. "I miss him already, but you're right. Let's use our time wisely and make a plan for what happens next."

Sheena snorts a laugh. "Can't wait to see how this one gets fucked up."

We laugh, and things are better. Not good, but better.

CHAPTER TWENTY-ONE

Nothing like opening your mouth and letting your inner asshole out. I'm through the hotel lobby and into the rental car before I really catch my breath.

But when I do...*fuck.*

I rake my hands through my hair, appalled by my own stupidity. Part of me wants to turn things around and make it Trajan's mistake. Why would he agree to such a drastic step?

The rest of me wants to kick that selfish part in the balls.

Your vampire boyfriend spent weeks fighting off his maker's command that he kill you. Now he's found a way out and you shit on him. Real cool, MacPherson. Really fucking cool.

I pull the car out onto the access road that'll take me to the freeway, although I don't have an actual destination in mind. The light ahead of me turns red. Slowing to a stop, I grab my phone and open the maps app. Redondo Beach doesn't look too far. I aim for Sepulveda and drive south.

I find a place to park and head for the water. This isn't the remote, isolated area I'd hoped for. The strip, with its many shops and restaurants, has enough neon to see from space. Once I hit sand, I put the lights behind me and take off, walking so fast it's almost a run.

No matter how far I go, though, the traffic and noise hang on. I finally pick a lifeguard tower at random, climb to the top, and sit facing the water. The tide is high and the steady pulse of the waves soothe me. I try to empty my mind in hopes the answer will come to me if I'm not thinking about it.

I've been romantically involved with a vampire for years, but tonight, I balked at his desire to do something that's basic to his nature.

Vampires aren't born, they're made, but when Trajan said he intended to turn someone, I made a derogatory comment about his existence.

He's not going to forgive that easily, and I can't blame him.

The thing that really twists the knife is that he agreed to do it to keep from killing me. Guilt spreads over me like a damp blanket and again I try to let my thoughts go.

Doesn't work any better this time.

I watch the waves recede, trying to work out a way back to that godawful hotel room. I would apologize—of course I would apologize—and if—*if*—Trajan forgives me, I'll ask a few questions about this task he's given himself. From there we can discuss our general approach to getting Betancourt and how to save the Princess.

All that assumes I can climb down from this chair.

"I'm so sorry, *mo shíorghrá*. I should never have implied…no." I mumble the words to the water. "Try again. I'm sorry, *mo shíorghrá*. I'm honored that you'd take this on for me, but…Not that, either."

I let my head tip back so I'm staring up into the heavens. "Come on, MacPherson. You're made of stronger stuff than this."

At least I think I'm made of stronger stuff. There's only one way to find out.

I climb down and trudge through the sand. People are partying on the lanai of a restaurant named Tony's. Their raucous laughter could be aimed directly at me. I deserve to be laughed at. Hell, I deserve more than that. Hoping I don't make things worse, I head for the car.

I'm still hoping when I reach the hotel. I knock on the door to our room, even though I have the key. David calls "Hello" through the door, and I answer.

"It's me. Connor. I'd like to talk to you if I could."

David swings the door open. "Took you long enough." He stands aside and for a moment I hesitate. I'm always apologizing for shit. At some point Trajan's going to run out of patience with me.

I just have to hope he hasn't reached that point yet.

I enter and realize it's just the three of us. "Where's, uh, Sheena and…the new girl?"

"Cliffe's going to sleep in the guest room at Sheena's for the time being," Trajan says. His aura is a cool blue, at odds with his rumpled trousers and button-down. His aura isn't usually so clear and I blink to make sure I'm not seeing things. The blue stays the same, a pretty contrast to David's golden aura.

David has a flowered sarong tied around his hips and a sleeveless mesh top that shows off his biceps and pecs and both my men look so good I'm afraid of what'll come out if I open my mouth.

"Are you okay?" David asks. "We were worried when you took off like that."

Of course they'd worry about me. No way I deserve having these two men in my life. "I'm sorry. Sorry you were worried, sorry I took off, and profoundly sorry I hurt you, Trajan." I close the gap between us, staring straight into the depths of his dark eyes. "I'm sorry, *mo shíorghrá.* You deserve better than that from me."

"This is one of the rare occasions when I would have preferred a lie to the truth."

His words are harsh, but his tone is kind. He takes hold of my hand and rubs his thumb over the thin skin on the underside of my wrist. "I'm so sorry," I whisper, earning a grimace.

"I know, *amore mio*, but next time let's not do anything worth apologizing for." He pulls me into an embrace and I go willingly, gratefully, relieved beyond measure that he might forgive me.

"That's right. Kiss and make up," David says, and I fully support his directness. I want to put my lips on Trajan, to wrap my body around him, to feel his cool skin and breathe in his dusty vampire scent.

"I will do whatever it takes to rid myself of Jacques Betancourt. You are safe from me, Connor. I will never obey my maker again."

"And I'll do whatever I can to help."

David slides between us. "We've gone days without seeing each other. I want, no, I need to be close to you both."

Amused by his declaration, I wrap an arm around his waist. "I'm not sure we have time for what you have in mind."

"We absolutely do." He grabs my wrist and reaches for Trajan. "We don't have to have sex, but I want all three of us in a puppy pile before we do anything else."

Trajan and I share a glance over David's head. "Can you?" I ask. Trajan closes his eyes, his lips compressed.

"How long has it been since you fed?" David's question is gentle, but he hasn't let go of either of us.

"I hit up a hospital for some blood earlier this evening."

David gags. "You need to feed properly. Come on, both of you. We've got at least an hour before sunrise."

"Oh, I should probably tell you—"

"You can tell me anything you want, Guido, when we're in bed." David spins away from us, loosening the sarong and letting it fall. The shirt follows, and the sight of his bare ass disappearing through the doorway is all the motivation I need. Trajan's already on his way and damned if his shirt doesn't hit the floor before he goes through the doorway.

I hold back, not because I don't want them, but because I do. I'm reluctant to test Trajan with Jacques still in play.

"Hey, Snoop, get in here." There's enough command in David's tone to nudge me toward the door.

"Who's Snoop?" Trajan asks.

"Had to come up with a new one because we met a real phouka and I owe Connor an apology for every time I called him Pookie."

Trajan's laugh sounds so normal I can't stop myself, leaving a trail of clothing on my way. The room's not any bigger than the front room, with barely enough space to walk around the queen-sized bed. A lamp is on the narrow nightstand near Trajan's head, but it can't have more than a 20-watt bulb. David's in the middle of the bed, propped against Trajan, who's sitting upright. I get in on the opposite side from Trajan and roll onto my side, draping a leg across David's calves.

We're quiet for a while, and though at first I don't think it's possible, my mind does slow down. The steady rhythm of their breathing soothes me. If Trajan's bothered by my nearness, he doesn't let it show.

"This," David says on a sigh. "Pack needs to stick together."

"I'm sorry." Trajan's voice is soft, but there's a core of strength there. "I couldn't get rid of his voice in my head."

"He's still there?" David asks. I'm too busy holding my breath to speak.

"Yes, but I'm getting better at tuning him out."

David twists around so he can give Trajan a raised eyebrow. "What changed?"

"Me."

I'm pretty damned sure there's more to this story, but as the King of Secrets, I'm in no place to demand a full recount. David teases his fingers through my hair and his touch brings such comfort it chases away all other thoughts.

"So, about Cliffe," Trajan says after a while. That makes David stiffen, and not in a fun way.

"I can't believe you brought her here, with all the shit that's going on."

"She's a psychic and when we first met, she said something that could be pertinent to our current situation."

David sits up and crosses his legs, hunching over on his forearms. "So you decided to dump her into the middle of a vampire war?"

"I want to know what else she has to say," Trajan says.

"That seems like kind of a stretch." David chews on his lower lip for a while and finally nods. "At any rate, a wolf should have a pack. I'll introduce her to Lydia. That is, assuming the Los Angeles Were Authority doesn't slam me into werewolf jail."

"What the hell are you talking about?" Trajan asks.

I scoot closer to David, putting more of my skin on his. "He got a summons. Someone complained about his unauthorized pack."

"I mean, it's not as serious as Uncle Brendan last spring, but they could try and separate us if they wanted to be assholes about it."

"Good luck with that." I run a hand along David's thigh. "As far as I can tell, you weren't supposed to be able to make a pack with us, so I don't see how they can undo what shouldn't have been done in the first place."

David pokes me in the shoulder. "Go on with your twisty logic. I didn't say they'd be able to separate us, just that they might try."

"Your father saw what we'd done, and he didn't complain. Tell him to shut them up."

Trajan's idea makes sense, but I understand David's frown, too.

"Nah," David says. "I've made it this far without playing the son-of-the-American-Alpha card. I'll just show up at the assigned time and explain things using language aimed at the sixth-grade level to be sure they understand."

"Sounds good," I say, but I make a mental note to text David's sister Abby and see if she can play the American Alpha card on his behalf.

There's a limit to the amount of bullshit a person should have to deal with.

David slides down between us, tugging Trajan with him. We shift around so he's got his head on my shoulder with Trajan stuck to his other side.

David reaches up to pull the hair away from his neck and tilts his head to bare more of his throat.

"You really drank hospital blood?" he says, grinning.

I hold my breath, wondering if Trajan's going to take him up on his invitation. His big body is relaxed, so whatever he'd figured out to shut Jacques up must be working but feeding puts him in a fairly vulnerable state.

I'm not sure whether or not I wanted him to risk it.

Trajan slides a finger along the line of David's jaw. "God, you smell good, puppy."

David snickers. "Vanilla sage body wash and ginger pomade."

"And wolf." Trajan's voice has gone husky and my cock starts to get thick. Leaning over David, Trajan traces his jawline with his tongue. I barely stifle a groan. David arches his back, his throat exposed. Trajan hums softly, leaning closer, and then he bites.

David's gasp is the most erotic sound ever. Trajan sucks at the wound on his throat, one hand sliding down David's belly. He wraps his fingers around David's cock. I take myself in hand. Trajan strokes, and so do I, and between us, David writhes.

I don't know how far I should let this go. David's blazing toward an orgasm and Trajan's caught up in the act of feeding. My cock is throbbing, but we're surrounded by enough crazy that one of us should pay attention.

David reaches for my dick, wrapping his hand over mine, and all my good intentions get lost in a wave of pleasure. Trajan takes my hand and draws it to his lips. He wraps his tongue around my index finger, sending chills across my skin. I close my eyes. He scratches the tip of my finger across one of his incisors. Pleasure swirls down my arm and he moves to my palm, planting a soft kiss.

I'm breathing hard, but so is he. Between us, David mumbles something about fucking. Trajan strokes him faster and in about a minute David shouts about coming.

He thrashes between us, his thick release spilling over the vampire's hand. Trajan lies still, his head propped on his hand. After a few more gentle pulls, I bank my desire, too. David's release seems to be enough for both of us.

Trajan and I share a glance. His eyes are darker than normal, nearly black, and I sense a new sort of strength in the clarity of his aura.

As always, his undead nature calls to mine. Death is a thing we share in an essential way, holding us together as tightly as the bonds the wolf has created.

"David was right." Trajan's still covering David's junk with his big hand.

David rubs his cheek against Trajan's shoulder. "Of course I am," he says, slurring his words.

"We needed this." He pauses. "I needed this."

I want to kiss him, but I'm afraid. Jacques' command hangs between us, more lightly than before but still present. "I needed it too," I say, although *need* is an inadequate term. Physical closeness with David and Trajan has the strength of a demand, the unrequited hunger found in yearning. The details of them—David's all-over tanned skin and smile that never quite fades, Trajan's unruly hair and quiet strength—are things I'll never forget, yet I cannot go long without experiencing them.

This thing we share exceeds anything I'd ever expected, and I will do anything in my power to preserve it.

Anything.

David makes a sound that's close to a snore and, as if reading my mind, Trajan pokes him. "Don't fall asleep. We have to figure out our next moves."

"Don't wanna move." David grabs hold of each of us and drags us closer.

Gently disentangling himself, Trajan says, "I know, puppy."

David groans, stretching his arms over his head and pointing his toes.

I pull out my phone. "We've got a few things on the calendar." I open the app. "You meet with Delia Packard tonight, David's got an appointment with the Were Authority tomorrow morning, and at some point Jacques is going to attempt to bring Armageddon down on our heads."

"Sounds about right."

David's still stretching, although now he's bent over with his nose to his knees. "The Were Authority thing is a huge pain in the ass."

"I'll be there to represent your pack, and so will Cliffe. We can ask Sheena to back us up, too."

"Yeah." David sounds bummed, but I don't know how to cheer him up, so I change the subject.

"It's kinda fucked that we don't know Jacques' schedule."

David straightens, bending a knee and hooking it with his opposite elbow, twisting his upper body. "Connor and I had an enlightening discussion with the Morrigan and a phouka who works for Jacques. Whatever he's planning involves the Princess and black magic."

Trajan's brows are drawn together. "The vampire sires in this area are concerned that he's going to bring the elves down on all our heads."

"And both Sheena and Lydia say he's gathering allies to him," I say. "I wonder what that means, exactly."

David unwinds and when a phone starts to buzz in the other room, he gets up. His toned legs and perfectly molded ass give my cock ideas, but the look on his face when he comes back to the bedroom hits me like a bucket of cold water.

"Friday the tenth." He frowns at the phone. "The dude I bought the warded hacky sack from needs a werewolf bodyguard on Friday because he's heard there's a big black magic thing happening and he and a few others are going to try to stop it."

Trajan and I share a glance. "Sounds like we have a date," Trajan says.

"Like, in three days."

"*Damnú*. Now we just need to know where it's happening and how many people we're going to be fighting."

David's attention is still on his phone. "The witches are still trying to divine the location, according to Albion Bird. As to how many we're fighting, maybe we should check out the place Betancourt's been staying. With luck he'll have his evil minions camped in the yard so we can count them."

I doubt it'll be that easy. Things are coming to a head, and we need to be ready.

CHAPTER TWENTY-TWO

Trajan

Connor, David and I pile into the rented SUV. We have a good four hours until midnight and we're all too antsy to sit in a hotel room. Instead our destination is the house in the Santa Monica hills where they believe Jacques is staying. Connor drives and David keeps the mood light. I spend most of the trip repeating "get out get out get out" because my maker's presence is hovering on the edge of my awareness, waiting for the slightest opening.

We take the 101 and traffic is surprisingly light. Eight p.m. is still rush hour in this part of the world.

"The house is at the end of a long driveway," Connor says, "so we can't really drive past without calling a whole lot of attention to ourselves. We'll have to park and walk in. Poke around a little and see what we see."

"Poke." David demonstrates by jabbing Connor in the shoulder.

Connor laughs. "Yeah, that."

Their lightness helps, for a moment, but soon I'm back to *get out get out get out*.

We go from freeway to four-lane surface street to two lane to gravel road. We come to a turn out and Connor pulls into it, parking the car behind a cluster of live oaks. There's a stone fence along the side overlooking the ocean, and I stand there for a minute, taking in the view.

Get out get out get out. Jacques' presence is even more insistent, as if proximity is giving him strength. Connor's in no danger; I'm not fighting the urge to harm him as much as I'm fighting to keep my thoughts to myself.

And this is a battle I will win.

The unwritten vampire code treats sires as equals. There may be differences in power—age and gifts see to that—but if a vampire is strong enough to create more of our kind, they're accorded a certain level of respect. Delia Packard has found a loophole in me. She can solve the problem of Jacques and if I'm successful, I'll be on equal footing with him.

Becoming a sire has never been a goal of mine. Keeping Connor safe and Jacques out of my head are their own incentive.

"How far is it?" David asks.

Connor points up the gravel road. "A couple hundred feet. It's the only house we'll come to."

"Is it warded?"

He shrugs. "If there were wards on it last time, we plowed right through them. Brodie and I tangled with a couple of guards, so we should probably stick together."

We wear black clothing and David has a knit cap pulled over his bleached blond hair. With Connor in the lead, we head up the driveway.

I don't mean to fall behind, but something slows me, some weight I don't know I carry. The road is unlit, except by the moon, which seems to dim until I can't see Connor or David at all.

The person next to me, however, is plainly visible.

Jacques Betancourt strides up the gravel drive beside me. His reliance on a glossy black cane doesn't slow him at all. In his other hand, he carries a large white cloth, spotted with blood. I don't say anything, and after the first glance, I don't look at him.

Get out get out get out.

"It won't work, you know." If he's at all out of breath, it doesn't show in his voice. I don't respond, fully focused on taking one step and then the next. The air itself weighs me down, as if I'm covered in a blanket of rock.

"You're not strong enough. You never have been."

His words sting, burrowing deep in my consciousness. Still, I ignore him, though my footsteps slow.

"I made you and I will destroy you." Jacques stops, and to my frustration, so do I.

"Why?" I ask finally, giving voice to that frustration, and something more. A sense of betrayal. "For one hundred and fifty years I've done anything you asked me to. Why do you want to destroy me now?"

"Don't be stupid. You've defied me. I asked you for one simple thing, to get rid of the one who threatened me, who threatened us both, and you refused. I have no choice but to punish you."

"Punish and destroy are different things. Besides, Connor is no danger to you."

Jacques gives a cold laugh. "You're right about that. I've gone past the point where he can hurt me. I may have one more surprise for him, however."

In all of this, he hasn't coughed once. If he's not really here, then I've been talking to myself. "What surprise?"

"If I tell you, it won't be a surprise." He flutters his fingers at me. "But know this. You won't live to defy me again, and I'll take down your little wolf pack, too."

"Really?" I say, feigning shock. At the same time, I think *Go Away* with as much energy as I can muster, and it works.

Jacques Betancourt disappears.

So does the layer of darkness that had wrapped around us, and so does the heaviness in the air. Connor and David are standing at the edge of a lawn. "You okay?" Connor pitches his voice low.

"Yeah."

"The house has motion sensor lights on each corner," David says, "and there seems to be a lot of activity inside."

I reach them. If they think it's odd that I arrived late, they don't show it. "How can you tell?"

"Lights turning on and off." Connor gestures toward the house, where on cue, the light in a big window blinks out.

"And lots of silhouettes, people moving around," David adds.

A new light flashes on, accompanied by a surge of raucous laughter. A trio of dark figures spills out of an open door and heads around the house.

"The back yard is terraced." Connor's attention is on the place the figures disappeared. "I think there's a pool on one of the levels, although we got disinvited before we had a chance to do more than take a quick look."

"Disinvited." David snickers.

"That sounds painful," I say, trying to shake off the cold fear Jacques left me with. I wish I knew whether it was my command that got rid of him, or if he'd have left anyway.

"What we need is someone on the inside to tell us how many are in there."

"Someone like Dash Dolivo?" David gives Connor a speculative look.

Connor pivots so he's facing the house. "I wonder if he's in there."

"We could ask your…Morrigan."

Connor rolls his shoulders, laughing softly. "There are a whole lotta ways that could end, and most of them are bad."

The door opens again. "We're too exposed right here," I say.

Someone is coming. Someone we don't want to see. I take a step in the direction of the car. "Come on."

David inhales sharply. "Werecat." He moves, too.

"We haven't really learned anything." Connor's standing at the corner of the lawn. I don't see anyone else, but the air carries a pungent odor, and if David says it's a werecat, I believe him.

"Come on," I say, my voice little more than a hiss.

"But—" Connor's cut off when a huge grey cat the size of a panther launches itself across the lawn and lands at his feet. Connor's got both hands out when he should be going for his gun.

A second werecat lopes up. It's just as large as the first one; its coat is coal black and long fangs curve down from its upper jaw.

With a curse about ruining perfectly good jeans, David shifts. His wolf is the size of those cats and to my ear, his growl is more threatening. Connor's still holding his hands out, locked in a stare down with the first werecat. "I'm going to shift, too," he says, "and when I do, I want you to run."

Not likely. "Sure."

"I mean it, Trajan. David and I'll each take a cat, and you get to the car and get it started."

That makes slightly more sense. With a lightning-quick move, Connor tosses me the keys. They land at my feet, and by the time I scoop them up, there's a thickly-muscled draft horse where Connor had been standing.

David and the black werecat are circling each other. The cat howls and feints, but David doesn't react. He's ready when the werecat pivots and leaps at him. They come together in a fury of teeth and flashing claws. Blood sprays, although I can't identify the source. David gives a sharp, barking growl and lunges.

The werecat springs out of his path. Both of them are bloody. Both of them are breathing hard. Connor and the other werecat are locked in an awkward dance, the big horse proving to be just as fast and nearly as agile. I'm torn between making sure my lovers are safe and getting us all out of there.

The confrontation has drawn the attention of the three who'd come out earlier. They come from behind the house at a jog, hollering at each other in one of the Slavic languages. Strigoi. Undead like vampires, they don't survive as long and retain less of their memory and intelligence.

Perfect fodder for a war.

"Come on," I shout, striding toward the car with my attention still on the ongoing fights. Connor has his werecat pinned with one heavy hoof, but David. *David.* He's tangled with the black werecat, and for a moment he falters. The cat locks its jaw on his shoulder, its rear paws clawing at David. If the thing gets its claws into his belly, David could be seriously injured.

Or worse.

The strigoi are closing in. David swipes at the werecat but the thing doesn't let go of its grip on his shoulder. Connor must see the strigoi—his head is up, ears alert. He dips his head, then kicks the pinned werecat in the head. The thing goes limp, and he makes a run at the strigoi.

They scatter, still heading in our direction but coming from different angles. David lets his legs go soft, catching the werecat off guard. The cat's jaw loosens and David gives a mighty thrust with all four legs. He's free of the werecat, and now he's the aggressor.

I can't leave. Not without knowing both of them are safe. Connor's playing pinball with the strigoi, darting from one to the other, threatening them with his hooves and teeth. If I had a gun, I'd take aim at the cat David's fighting, but my only weapons are my speed and my strength.

David's moving more slowly, but he lunges at the cat, getting his teeth into the loose skin at the back of its neck. The werecat screeches and claws, but David manages to pin it to the dirt. He locks his jaw and shakes. There's a crack, and the werecat goes still.

Connor gallops over, rolls of foamy sweat sliding over his graceful neck and shoulders. I don't wait to see if the strigoi have given up, but trusting that Connor will keep David safe, I run for the car.

Now we have a better idea of what we're up against. Jacques has called shifters to him and has managed to create strigoi. That's in addition to his vampire children and any number of other supernaturals.

Connor may not like it, but I need to turn the human. I won't be able to fight Jacques any other way.

Rolling Hills Estates might be the least likely name for a vampire's lair ever. When I think of rolling hills, I see a woman in a dirndl spinning and singing about how the hills are alive. There's too much sunshine for one of us.

Traffic was abysmal, even by LA's standards. The map said we were traveling twenty miles. Reality said it would take us over an hour to get there. Between the battle with the werecats, the battle with traffic, and the battle with the security guard at the gate—the whole town of Rolling Hills is fenced in to keep the riffraff out—we arrive at exactly two minutes to midnight. That's going to have to be close enough.

Madame Packard's house is a comfortable Mediterranean style, with bougainvillea and ivy covering the white plaster walls. We park in the driveway behind a black Rolls Royce, and before we get out of the car, Connor takes hold of my arm.

"You sure?" The tension thrumming through him ratchets up my own. If I say "No," he'll have us back on the road before I can catch my breath.

"Yes." Because my doubts are my own.

David's sitting in the middle of the rear seat. He leans forward and covers Connor's hand with his. He doesn't say anything but the contact helps settle me.

"Come on, Cliffie." Sheena opens the door behind me. She and Cliffe get out, giving the three of us some privacy. We don't really need it. I've heard Connor's arguments and he's heard mine, and as usual, David's the link holding us together.

"We should go." My voice is rough. I glance from one of them to the other. "If things don't go as I hope they will, I want you to get out sooner than later. Don't engage. Leave me to deal with Madame Packard and her crew."

Connor's sharp indrawn breath is his only response.

"Guido, Guido, Guido." David squeezes my arm. "We're with you come hell or pissed-off vampire. Now let's do this."

The moment ends and we climb out of the rental car. With David at my right hand and Connor at my left, we cross the manicured lawn to the front door. We'd stuck with the all-black color scheme, with Cliffe and David leading the

Goth brigade. Sheena and Connor look chic. I look somber.

The doorbell triggers a musical chime and we don't have to wait long before the woman from the restaurant, Gillian, opens it.

She clasps her hands in front of her chest, her smile the very definition of delight. She's dressed in a long, wine-colored gown and her curls are held away from her face with a slender gold band. "You did come! I was afraid you'd change your mind."

I was afraid of that, too. Not because I have any philosophical objection to creating another vampire but because I'd never acknowledged my own power in that way. If Madame Packard is wrong and I fall short of what's needed, things could go very badly. The man will die and likely so will I.

But if I do meet my final death, Jacques won't be able to give me orders and Connor will be safe. And with or without me, I trust Connor to save the Princess and stop Jacques' ultimate plan.

I reach out and Gillian clasps my hand. "I'm honored to take part in something so meaningful."

Gillian's eyes grow damp with light pink tears. "Come in, please."

Still holding my hand, she leads us inside. The marble entryway opens into a series of rooms.

The one Gillian leads us to is small and cozy, with a small fire in the fireplace, thick carpet on the floor, and a large window with a view of downtown LA.

Madame Delia Packard is ensconced in the center of a large, L-shaped sofa. The bearded vampire who'd been with her at the restaurant sits next to her, his glower a sharp contrast to Gillian's happiness. A human man sits alone in an upholstered chair, the kind that reclines with a lever on the side.

"Welcome, Trajan Gall." Madame Packard lifts her hand and I bend over it, pressing a kiss to her cold flesh. "I'm so pleased you're here."

If she notices that my entourage outnumbers hers, she doesn't let on. No doubt she can draw on unseen resources if necessary, a theory I do not want to test. Sheena and Cliffe stay in the doorway while Connor and David stick close to my side. Gillian perches on the human's lap, running her fingers through his hair.

"I don't think you've met my companions," I say and at Madame Packard's expectant nod, I make introductions.

"I remember your wolf," she murmurs, "and I'm most pleased to make the acquaintance of a member of the Elites. And an Amazon! It amuses me that you have such powerful friends but shy away from your own power."

I manage a smile. "The issue never came up." *What power?* My interests are in business and in Connor and David, not necessarily in that order. I'd never sought power for its own sake, but with a slow breath, I set aside my nerves and resolve to take it now.

"I imagine Betancourt preferred to have you in thrall rather than set you free."

My smile freezes in place. "I wouldn't have said he kept me in thrall. Our arrangement worked well, until…"

"Until he pushed you too far." Her expression grows cold. "He's pushing all of us too far with this idiotic spell. Tatiana may have been estranged from her family, but the elves will still avenge her death, and we'll all pay for it.

"I'm not particularly generous, Trajan Gall, nor do I do favors easily. You're a weapon, nothing more. I do not want to be staked in my bed by an enraged elf, and the best way to stop Betancourt is to have his oldest scion take him on, so" — her expression lightens — "please make Gillian happy by turning her lover."

I turn to the man in question. Gillian is curled around him, her smile so bright it's almost painful. My own nerves have me ready to crawl out of my skin, but it's too late to turn back. I meet the man's gaze, probing lightly to make sure he's sober and uninfluenced by others.

"What's your name?" I ask.

"Peter."

I introduce myself, figuring if we're going to reach the level of intimacy it'll take to turn him, we should at least be on a first name basis. "And Peter, what do you understand about what we're doing here?"

"You're going to turn me so I can spend eternity with my beloved."

His flowery language feels coached, but I don't get a sense that he's anything other than sincere. "That's right. I'm going to drain the blood from your body and at the moment of death, I'll give you some of mine. You will feel pain, although you will not recall the sensations that come with dying and being reborn."

"I'll be right here with you, my darling." Gillian nuzzles his ear. "We'll endure this together."

I give the man one more long look. His calm helps me, and I motion for him to recline the chair. He does and Gillian stretches out next to him, spooning him from behind. I keep my gaze on the pair of them. Looking at Connor will undo me. It's enough that he and David are nearby. A palpable sense of their presence grounds me.

"Because we're pack." David's voice sounds in my head, words for me alone. I close my eyes and I can see him, holding onto me with one hand and

Connor with the other. They're with me, but this is something I must do alone.

"All right, Peter. Let's begin."

I raise his chin with one finger, bending low over him and, picking a spot over his jugular vein, I bite.

This isn't feeding for nutrition's sake. This is purposeful, so I continue long past satiation. My fears and doubts grow quieter with every swallow and soon, all I'm tuned to is the rhythm of my suck and the beat of his heart.

A beat that grows slower, and slower still.

His spirit wavers. Now. It is time. I slash my thumbnail across my palm and press it to his mouth.

He lies still, the time between each heartbeat growing longer. *Oh fuck, I'm not enough. Delia is wrong.* "Come on." I squeeze blood from my palm. It trickles over his lips and reaches his tongue. His heart stops. Silence. One long swell of nothing. I squeeze harder. *I have to be enough.* "You must drink."

Gillian cries out, slapping his cheek. "Drink, Peter. Please."

I press my palm more firmly to his lips and reach down with my other sense to catch hold of his spirit. "Stay."

I'm not sure if I say the word out loud, but his heart beats again, once, twice. He gasps and grabs hold of my wrist with hands that feel like claws. He drinks, Gillian sobbing on his shoulder. I let him go until some instinct tells me he's had enough. I pull away, though he scrabbles after me.

His eyes are open, vampire black. "Rest now," I say, holding my wounded palm against my chest. He exhales, falling into Gillian's embrace.

I turn to face the others in the room. "It is done."

I've created a vampire scion, just as Jacques had done to me, and someone else had done to Jacques. The line of us stretches far into the past, and I'm both humbled and proud to take my place. And for the first time since this debacle began, I no longer hear Jacques' voice in my head.

At all.

CHAPTER TWENTY-THREE

CONNOR

The room stinks of power. Most of it comes from Madame Delia Packard, who gives the impression that she's amused by the four of us who accompanied Trajan. Her reasons for asking him to do this deed are clear enough—everyone wants a piece of Betancourt—but I still don't trust her.

Trajan straightens slowly, as if he's feeling every year he's been on this earth. The new vampire, Peter, clamors about being hungry. Trajan steps aside and Gillian takes her lover to another room, where presumably there's a food source.

"Keep an eye on him," Madame Packard calls after her. "Don't let him drain anybody."

"Of course, Madame." Gillian laughs, and I don't want to think about any of this too hard.

David is the first to reach Trajan. I hang back because I'm not sure of the reception I'll get. They murmur together, and Trajan assures David he's okay. When Trajan looks up and catches my eye, the last of my doubts fade.

Trajan Gall has reached for power and claimed it.

Sheena leaves her post in the doorway and wraps an arm around Trajan's shoulders. They share a long glance, as if Sheena's repeating David's questions without putting them into words. Once he's reassured her, Trajan turns to me.

"Okay, *amore mio*? I think it's time to go."

I nod, unable to speak. The weight of our baggage, our hits and our misses, is almost too heavy to bear.

"Thank you, Trajan Gall. You have made Gillian very happy, which makes me very happy." Madame Packard is still seated, the bearded vampire still at her side like a sullen sentry.

"Madame Packard." Trajan bows in her direction. He's got David under one arm and Sheena under the other. "Unless there's anything else, we'll leave you to your evening."

"You can find your way out, yes?"

He assures her we can, and I make a break for the door. I tuck my arm through Cliffe's because the poor girl looks like she's seen a ghost and make a beeline for the car.

The ride back is fairly silent. Cliffe is in front with me so Trajan doesn't have to let go of David and Sheena. Cliffe's worrying a bracelet, as if she needs to keep her hands busy and that's the only thing available. "Don't suppose I can smoke?" she ask, pitching her voice low.

"I heard that." David sounds a little drunk. "And this is a no-smoking zone."

"Hmmph." Cliffe goes back to her bracelets and I go back to navigating traffic.

We get to the hotel in a lot less time than it took us to get to Madame Packard's. I park, but before we get out, Sheena claps a hand on Cliffe's shoulder. "You're coming with me, right?"

Cliffe gives her a shy smile. "That'd be great."

Sheena's next question is for me. "Tomorrow we meet to plan our next steps?"

"Yeah. We could do it tonight, but…"

Sheena laughs hard at that. "You really are clueless."

Ignoring her, I open the door and get out. Sheena and Cliffe take off; Cliffe talking about how she's studied krav maga and would be happy to help us fight. My feet are apparently stuck to the pavement and only when David comes over and loops his arm through mine can I move.

If the car ride was quiet, those six floors on the elevator are like hiding in a tomb. Even David's got a faraway look in his eye, as if he's imagining life without our threesome.

Because honestly, after the way I doubted him, Trajan would be within his rights to kick me to the curb.

David's the first one to the door. He swipes the keycard and heads in. I'm the last one through. I can't seem to take more than a step or two. It's like I'm waiting for the ax to fall or something.

Trajan's got his back to me. He does something that makes David smile, then spins around. He slams me against the door, his forearm jammed under my chin. "You," he says. Our gazes clash and hold.

And he kisses me.

He's hungry and oh, so strong. He jams a knee between my legs and the pressure of his arm against my throat makes me light-headed. His mouth demands entrance and I open to him. He tastes different, as if I'm kissing a stranger, but that doesn't stop me from kissing him back.

We writhe together, and when he tires of my mouth, he works his way down my throat. His fangs scratch my skin, and though he nips, he doesn't bite. I rock my hips on his thigh and he growls. The rough sound lights me up and I need to feel his skin against mine.

It's been so long since we were this close. I lose sight of what he deserves and what I should have done and get lost in the sensation of his big hard body next to mine.

My leather jacket slides off my shoulders and he rips my shirt down the middle. That makes David laugh, but with Trajan latched onto my throat and manhandling me out of my clothes, I can't do much more than smile.

"Want you," he says, another growl that cranks me up higher than the first.

"Oh, I want you so much," I manage to gasp.

"Come here." He yanks at my arms, pulling me toward one of the beds. Letting go long enough to take off his own shirt, he shoves me down and falls on top of me.

His bare chest presses against mine, the dark hair across his pecs creating another source of friction. He kisses me again, so deep it's like our souls are bound, and when he pulls away, we both gasp.

"Puppy needs some attention, too."

I nod, my vision blurred.

"Get your pants off and get on your hands and knees."

His voice carries a new level of command. I do as I'm told, unable to do otherwise. Once I get my pants off, Trajan pushes me to the center of the bed. David's as naked as I am. He's propped the pillows against the headboard and his beautiful cock is right there for the taking.

I lean forward, forcing my ass into the air and nuzzling David's clean-shaven balls. Trajan jams a lubed finger into me with the same demanding energy he's done everything else. Yeah, it burns, but it's a good burn.

He works me open roughly while I try to keep from chomping on David's cock by mistake. The contrast between David's warmth and Trajan's cool touch is intoxicating. I lost track of anything but how I'm trapped between the two of them.

I never want to be anywhere else.

When Trajan trades his finger for the head of his cock, I let David slip from my mouth.

"That's right, Pookie. You bite me and I'll mess you up."

I glance at him and smile. His bleached hair is falling into his face and his eyes glow with pleasure. I nip his ballsack and he mock-swats my cheek.

Trajan forces his way into me in one motion and I have to close my eyes. I rest my forehead on David's belly, raising my hips further. Trajan pauses but not for very long. Before I'm truly ready for him, he drives himself deep.

The way my own cock starts to leak says I was ready for him after all.

Trajan sets a heavy rhythm and once I catch my breath, I draw the head of David's cock back into my mouth. I don't take him deep—I can't, not with Tray pounding on me—but I clasp his shaft in both hands and do what I can. I swear the vibrations Trajan is creating travel through me to David and he arches his back, driving himself deeper into my mouth.

I'm suspended between the two of them. David grabs me by the hair, pulling me closer. Trajan reaches for my cock. One tug. Two. A climax rips through me, catching me by surprise. I cry out. My body goes rigid. Pleasure swamps whatever's left of conscious thought and I fall into darkness.

I'm brought back by Trajan, his hips thrusting hard and fast. David's taken charge of his own dick, and he strokes in time with Trajan. His eyes are heavy with lust and soon he, too, goes over. I shut my eyes and his cum splatters over my chin and my throat.

"Come on, Guido, it's your turn now." David's grinning like some kind of debauched angel. Trajan grips my hips so hard I'm afraid he's going to tear holes in my skin and then he shouts.

His big body stiffens, his cock jammed in so deep I'll feel it next week. He holds that position for a long moment, then slumps over on top of me.

I end up between the two of them, all of us on a single queen-sized. It's tight, but I love the feel of them both. Trajan strokes my hair, murmuring *amore mio* this, *amore mio* that.

I don't know what I've done to be this lucky, but I vow to do everything in my power to save what we have.

CHAPTER TWENTY-FOUR

"What time is it?"

Connor answers from across the bed. "Almost eight thirty."

Fuckity fuck fuck fuck. "I have to be there by ten."

"Where?"

"The Were Authority, dumbass. Get up." Connor's agreed to come with me and no way am I going to let him weasel out. Trajan obviously can't. He retired to the vampire room after spending most of the early morning hours fucking us both senseless. I sling myself out of bed, wincing when my feet hit the floor. Yes, Tray did ride me hard, in the best possible way.

"You didn't make me coffee, Snoop," I say on my way into the bathroom.

"You don't drink coffee, idiot." He gives himself a good stretch, muttering about the nightmare that would be David Collins on caffeine.

He's not wrong.

I dress in what I like to call my colorful conservative look: jeans with no holes, shoes with no heels, and a button-down the color of melon sherbet. I pull my hair back into a restrained ponytail, twisting it so the strands of shocking pink don't show. A little eye liner but no mascara or blush and I'm good to go.

Connor's gone with a more conservative-conservative look including khaki trousers and a single-breasted jacket. Sheena drops Cliffe off and we find her in the lobby. She has a way of dressing that's designed to avoid attention, though I can't put my finger on how she does it. Which I guess is the point.

"All right," I say. "Let's do this."

We pile into the rented Ford — *OMG kill me now another Ford* — and Connor takes the wheel. He and Cliffe chat while I try to come up with a decent defense. I mean, the fact is, I didn't petition the Were Authority to be allowed to create a pack. It's not like I didn't know better, but I'd created a pack before I knew what I'd done.

I didn't plan it. I just reached out for the two closest sources of energy to keep myself from going crazy, and this is where we ended up.

The Were Authority offices are in Koreatown, in the kind of Art Deco building that gives LA its cool. We show up on time, not early and not late, and they're ready and waiting for us.

I could have asked Sheena to come, or maybe Lydia and some of her girls. Instead I have Connor and a girl named Cliffe-with-an-e. This might not end well.

We're ushered into a small courtroom. There's a judge sitting at an elevated desk with a stenographer at his right and an empty chair at his left. Three rows of chairs face the judge, and the walls are covered with photos of stern-looking weres.

Dad's photo is there, too, the biggest one of them all.

The judge introduces himself and asks me to step forward. In a sonorous voice, he reads the complaint against me.

"It has been brought to the attention of the Were Authority that you have created a pack and made yourself alpha without first applying for a permit, nor have you registered said pack with the appropriate governing bodies. What do you have to say?"

Connor's exasperated sigh has me pinching my lips to keep from giggling. *Not now, Collins. Keep your shit together.* "The complaint is correct, sir. I have created a pack without submitting any of the appropriate paperwork."

That comes out snarkier than I meant to, so I clear my throat, pulling myself together. "My pack is made up of Trajan Gall, vampire, and Connor MacPherson, Tuatha Dé Danann and former member of the Elites. Our newest member is" — *Oh shit what's her name?* — "Heathercliffe Mountbatten."

Connor and Cliffe stand on either side of me and damned if I can't feel the pull and swirl of pack surrounding us. It's not perfect — Trajan's not here — but it feels damned good. The judge is busy looking down his nose at us when there's a commotion from the main door.

"There's the asshole. He has no business starting a pack. None at all."

I glance over my shoulder and *yes it is* the fuckhead alpha of the Los Feliz pack. My teeth grind just a little, because he can't take my wolf in a fair fight but he sure can be a pain in my ass.

"Who are you?" The judge looks even less impressed than I am.

"I am alpha of the Los Feliz pack, James McMurtry."

"And you're the one who filed the complaint, Mr. McMurtry?"

If he notices the condescension in the judge's tone, ol' Jimbo ignores it. "Yes." He draws himself up in a painful display of misplaced pride. "When I learned of what he'd done, I found it offended my morals."

The judge's head tilted, ever so slightly. "Morals? You *are* a werewolf, aren't you?"

"I am, and I earned my position. What has he ever done?"

"He's got more balls than you ever will." A new voice speaks. A new, and familiar voice, one that knocks the breath out of my lungs.

My cousin Marcus Collins walks to the judge's desk. He's carrying a folder, and he looks like everything I once valued.

Except he's wearing a black patch over one eye.

I stare at the floor, unable to risk meeting his one-eyed gaze. His attention is on the judge, and he soberly opens the folder he's carrying. "David Collins is the oldest son of the American Alpha, Randolph Collins. He was wrongly cut out of the Collins Family pack, an act that will shame me until the day I die."

"You're a Collins?"

"Marcus, David's cousin."

Connor's got an arm around me and Cliffe is holding my hand. I'm shaking and it's all I can do not to give in to the tears that are threatening to fall. Marcus isn't just my cousin, he was my best friend. His participation in the act that got my uncle killed hurt me more than anything else.

Marcus hands the judge a piece of paper. "This is a letter from the American Alpha, authorizing the pack his son has created. Uncle Randolph knew about the pack from the beginning. He just didn't think anybody would be petty enough to file a complaint about something that's none of his goddamn business."

The last line is directed at the Los Feliz alpha, whose eyes are bright with anger.

Someone comes up behind me, wrapping me in a hug. I inhale and recognize my sister Abby's scent. I'd texted her to find out who filed the complaint, but this response well exceeds my expectations. I tip my head back and she presses her forehead between my shoulder blades. I don't get pack from her. The feeling is deeper, more essential.

Family.

"I think we're done here." The judge stands, and when the Los Feliz alpha starts shouting, the judge shuts him up with a snap of his fingers. "Clearly Mr. Collins' pack is authorized, and if you ever, and I mean *ever*, file a nuisance complaint again, I'll take a hard look at how you ended up in charge of anything, let alone a pack of wolves."

The judge leaves and so does the Los Feliz alpha, muttering about how he fought his way in and blah blah blah. Whatever. I wave at him, almost sad the dude didn't have the stones to challenge me. Showing him how a real wolf fights might have been fun.

For a minute or two.

Connor's standing close, and so are Cliffe and Abby. Marcus is a few feet away, staring at the floor.

"Thank you." My voice is so husky it's embarrassing.

"I meant what I said." Marcus doesn't sound like himself. He's distant, somber. Sad. "Going along with our uncle's plan is a shame I will carry for the rest of my life."

Yeah, well, it'll be on my mind, too. "What happened to your eye?"

He meets my gaze and his naked pain hits me with the strength of a blow. "Your father. He met with each of us who...I was one of the lucky ones."

"Oh." *I mean, what do you say to that?* I reach for Connor's hand, interlacing our fingers and squeezing tight. "Well, I appreciate your timely arrival today, and you too, Abby." I glance at my sister over my shoulder. Her closeness is restorative.

"Can you still fight?" Connor's shifted to Elites mode and the look he gives my cousin is far from friendly.

Marcus gives a one-shoulder shrug. "Not like I could, but I try."

"Because we have a bit of a situation and as long as you're in town, maybe you could help us out."

The flash of hope that crosses Marcus's face is hard to bear. "I could stick around. Yeah."

"Abby?" Connor raises his chin in my sister's direction.

"Of course."

He gives my hand a squeeze. "Okay?"

I don't even have to think about it. "Yeah."

"Come on, then. We meet this evening to come up with a plan."

With Connor in the lead, we leave the courtroom. It might not be possible for Marcus to regain my trust, but until half an hour ago, I'd had no idea he wanted to try.

CHAPTER TWENTY-FIVE

On rising, my focus is torn between what's happened in the past and what we still need to face. If I feel a pull toward Peter, the vampire I'd made, it is easily dismissed. Delia Packard will not shirk her obligation and her scion Gillian will see to his care.

Still, knowing that I'd taken that step gives me a newfound sense of responsibility, of confidence. That feeling lasts until I see my cell phone.

I have several text messages and at least three voicemails. All from Jacques. I read one of the texts.

What have you done?

I take a moment to reach out with all my senses. Weres, several of them, are in our hotel room, along with Sheena. Beyond that, darkness. Nothing from Jacques.

Nothing.

I check one of the voicemails. It's a wordier version of "What have you done" but with more expletives. I shrug and consider deleting the rest. His anger vibrates through the phone, but I no longer feel it vibrating through me.

Relief is tempered by an unexpected sense of loss. Jacques had been a part of me for so many years that I wondered what I'd do without him. Still, he should never have demanded that I kill Connor.

Connor, my lover, the only one who protested when I told him what I meant to do. *To bring someone else into the life you lead*…The memory of those words undercuts what's left of my relief. He'd apologized and of course I'd accepted his apology. I'd accomplished the "forgive," but I'm having trouble with the "forget" part of the equation.

In that unsettled state, I leave the vampire room. Connor and David are on one of the queen beds—Connor sitting upright with his back against the headboard and David sprawled across the foot. Sheena's claimed the only chair, and on the other bed, Cliffe, David's sister Abby, and a young man I don't recognize are jumbled together.

Well, Cliffe and Abby are curled up side-by-side, while the young man imitates Connor's posture, leaning against the headboard.

David gives me a lazy grin. "Hey, Guido, you need to comb your hair."

I palm the hair out of my face, taking stock of the situation. David's relaxed but wary, Connor's closed off, and the rest are doing a decent job of faking good humor. "What's going on?"

"David survived the Were Authority hearing," Connor says carefully. It's like he heard my forgive/forget monologue and is reluctant to call attention to himself.

"Yeah, but only because Marcus and Abby showed up."

Marcus? I must look puzzled, because David introduces his cousin to me. The young were is handsome enough, dark to David's dazzling gold. He's wearing an eye patch, and he barely flashes me a glance when David shares his name. I might recognize him from somewhere, but with so much going on, I'll deal with my half-memories later.

"So this is a celebration then?" Because, aside from a few In-N-Out burger wrappers and some bottles of water, the vibe didn't fit a party.

Sheena laughs. "It's a pack meeting."

"Of a sort," David says, rolling onto his back. He gives his belly a lazy scratch, his head tipped back so he can see the three weres on the other bed. "Now that we're officially official, we're discussing our membership requirements."

"Although we should probably table it for now," Connor says. "Melinda Barwell wants to meet with me in an hour. She's the Securitas Sensitive who agreed to help us find the Princess."

"She wants to meet with you in person?" David asks.

He shrugs. "We should probably split up, anyway. I can go to Headquarters to meet with her and you—"

"I'll come with you." Sheena's got one eyebrow raised in challenge. "Then the wolves can keep going with their pack meeting."

I glance from Connor to Sheena and back. "Should I come with you, too?"

"With any luck, Melinda will share the Princess's location. I can have Brodie meet me—"

"Us," Sheena interjects.

"*Us* at Headquarters, and from there we can go to Jacques' Malibu Hills house, see if we can get more of a head count."

"And the rest of us will stay here and, what?"

Connor's expression is still hard to read. "I figure you can go wherever it is Jacques is hiding the Princess's body and move it to someplace safe."

That makes a certain amount of sense. I gesture to the weres on the bed. "Are all of you in?"

"Of course." Abby speaks up first, but Cliffe and Marcus echo her agreement.

"It's what pack would do," Marcus adds.

David gives him a troubled look. "I'm not promising anything."

"I understand." Marcus's single eye is downcast. "All I ask for is a chance."

David closes his eyes and takes a measured breath. "Sure." The single word sounds close to a sigh. *I'm missing something here, and I better find out what before we bring more trouble down on our heads.*

Connor and Sheena get ready to leave. Connor and David kiss, while Sheena mock-punches Cliffe in the shoulder. On his way out the door, Connor squeezes my hand, and I'm not sure if I'm happy or sad he didn't lean in for a kiss. We might have fucked last night, but that doesn't mean all the hurts are healed.

I take Connor's spot on the bed with David. Marcus slides off the other bed and takes the chair, while Cliffe and Abby stretch out into the space he occupied. They're bickering over whether to watch a movie, but David finds an episode of *Dancing with the Stars* and pulls rank.

"You *are* the alpha, after all," Abby says, using the kind of little sister tone designed to get under David's skin.

David rests his head on my shoulder. "We're not that kind of pack. In his own way, Guido's more of an alpha than I'll ever be, and even though he hides it well, so is Pookie."

I snort a laugh. "Hides it well. I'm sure Connor would love that description."

"Just sayin'…"

"Well, you're my alpha," Cliffe says. She's cleaner than when we first met, and sitting next to Abby she's calmer, less brittle.

David winks at her and Cliffe's smile broadens.

"He's not my alpha." Abby blows him a kiss. "He's my big brother, which is worse."

Marcus stays silent and again I wonder what's not being said.

We watch forgettable television until Connor calls. The Sensitive has tracked Princess Tatiana to a cave on a beach. *Which one?*

"Sheena suggested you check out Leo Carillo Beach," Connor says. "That's the only one she knows that has a cave." I repeat the name out loud. David's attention goes to his phone and I assume he's hitting Google. Connor repeats the plan, that he, Sheena, and Brodie will head for Jacques' house, and we arrange to connect before sunrise.

We have our assignment. Find the cave. Find the Princess. And get the hell out.

CHAPTER TWENTY-SIX

"What do you think?" I murmur to Abby. We're crouched in the dirt behind a pile of driftwood between the parking lot and the beach. The Pacific keeps up its steady beat, the smell of dead fish competing with the salt air. Marcus and Cliffe are a few feet away behind their own rocks, and Trajan's off in the darkness on my left. Behind us the beach access road is quiet, but cars run along the Pacific Coast highway, their headlights flashing overhead. And behind that is darkness, where the Santa Monica mountains rise up from the coast.

The beach itself has been blocked off. Not that many people want to go to the beach after midnight, but there'll be some disappointed surfers here in a couple of hours.

Not that the No Trespassing signs are legal. The enormous pyre, cords of wood stacked five or six feet high, covering a ten-foot square between us and the water probably doesn't have a permit, either. Vampires don't play by the same rules as the rest of us.

"Looks like they all went home." Abby doesn't look at me, her attention still on the beach. "They must have this place warded somehow. I can't imagine they want anyone to find that thing."

It's not just wood. We've been here for over an hour, most of it spent watching a mixed bag of creeps and weirdos shove bundles of stuff in all the gaps. "If we get closer, we can smell what they've added to the pile."

"If we get closer, the guards we can't see now will find us."

She's not wrong. "Maybe we should shift first."

The moon gives me just enough light to see her roll her eyes.

"Okay, so we go on two legs, then."

I stand, waving at Cliffe and Marcus. The moon is bright enough that we don't need flashlights. "Let's check it out," I say, keeping my voice low and heading for the pyre.

After a single "tsk," Abby follows.

"Marcus, you go ahead of us." He has the sharpest nose, or he did. "And Abby, let us know if you feel any wards."

They couldn't just leave a pile of wood lying around for anyone to find. There must be wards in place to keep people away. I don't sense any magic, though. It's weird. It's…wrong.

Trajan materializes. "The cave is down past those rocks," he says, pointing to a mass of darkness jutting out into the water. Why would a vampire know his way around a beach? I decide I don't want to know.

A pinpoint of light marks a lifeguard tower. "Maybe whoever they've left guarding the place is in the cave with the Princess."

"We'll find out soon enough," Abby says. She's light on her feet, alert, and her presence soothes something I didn't know was raw. Marcus, too, bolsters me, despite the hurt between us. He's ten or fifteen feet ahead. He's not tall but he's always been broader than me. Now he's lanky, bony even. We haven't talked much since he'd shown up in the court room, but eventually we'll have to. Assuming I can forgive him.

Haven't decided yet. Trajan and Connor are my world, but family gives me something more. The fact that Dad let him live must mean something. I'm just not sure I want to know what.

With Trajan in the lead, we bypass the pyre, heading for the rocks. "The cave should be close."

Marcus and Cliffe stay on the beach. Trajan moves swiftly, navigating the uneven surface with more grace than I'm capable of. The rocks are rough, tide pools opening up between one step and the next. We reach a small patch of sand and Trajan points in the direction of a patch of darker darkness than the rest of the dark around us.

I take the lead here because the entrance to the cave is so low. I crouch, scooting along the sandy floor, until I'm able to straighten. Abby turns on the flashlight on her phone, a brave circle of brightness that gets swallowed by the dark too soon. I turn my flashlight on, too, and we head for the back of the cave.

Trajan passes us, but then he can probably see better than we can with our flashlights. "Here," he says, and I pick up my pace.

He's standing next to a regulation medical gurney. There are bits of seaweed stuck on the wheels and legs, as if the tide's been washing them a couple times a day, and there's a body on the bed. The body is wrapped in blankets, but even without seeing her face, I make an educated guess.

"It's her," Trajan says. "It has to be."

"How do we get her out of here?" Abby asks.

Trajan surveys the area. "Lifting her might trigger some kind of alarm, but I can't see us dragging this contraption across the rocks."

"Head out, and Abby and I will get her through the mouth of the cave."

"Not till we're sure lifting her doesn't trigger flying knives or something." Trajan lifts one of the blankets, revealing a trio of belts. One is buckled across her shoulders, one at her waist, and the other across her thighs.

"All right, Jacques," he murmurs. "How would you rig this?"

He unbuckles the belt at her legs and flinches. Nothing else happens. Abby gives a heavy exhale. She and I are standing out of the way, I hope.

Trajan unbuckles the other two belts, each time waiting for things to explode. Nothing happens. He gives her body an experimental lift, and nothing blows up.

"I can't decide if he's arrogant or just stupid," he says, catching my gaze. "I'll see you outside."

"Outside?"

"The tunnel's too small for both me and Tatiana. I'll go through and you bring her to me."

His idea makes as much sense as anything else, so we trade places and I slide my arms under the Princess's body. She's dead weight and not much warmer than the stone surrounding us. Abby leads the way with the lights from both our phones. When we reach the entrance, I get down on my knees and sidle out with the Princess still in my arms.

Trajan takes her from me, and we climb over the rocks to where we've left Cliffe and Marcus. The moon is brighter than my flashlight, so I shut it off and pocket my phone. We reach the beach. Marcus and Cliffe are in the shadows behind the pyre, waving frantically.

"Company," he hisses.

I pivot, damning my own stupidity. A row of figures stands between us and the beach access road. There's at least ten of them and there's not a friendly face in the bunch. "Fuck."

I knew it had been too easy.

"Take off," I say. I can't look at Trajan, but it's obvious what he has to do. "Get the Princess out of here."

Trajan goes very still, as if he's caught in some internal debate.

"Go now before they get any closer."

He shoots me a glance, one that says more than words. "Don't let any of them follow me, and don't get hurt."

With that, he's gone, running faster than any were could match. Assuming our new friends are weres and not vampires. One, a little guy on the end, takes off after him, moving human-fast.

"You heard what he said. Now shift." I bark the command and as fast as possible, I'm shoulder to shoulder with three wolves. Marcus yips, his muzzle pointed toward the guy who's gone after Trajan. I nod, and he takes off.

Cool cool. That leaves me, Abby, and Cliffe to take on eight or nine…whatever they are. Not human, I can tell that much.

Maybe it'd be smarter if we all ran after Trajan.

Things get blurry, fast. My wolf's vision is at once more acute and less coherent. Abby and Cliffe wait for my cue. *Because you're the alpha, dumbass.* I'm the alpha, and I've already sent two packmates off into who-knows-what danger. Some of our opponents have shifted, so now we're facing a couple of werecats, a bear, and a fierce hawk, who's perched on the shoulder of the one who might be their leader. With luck the others are strigoi, those charming vampire/zombie hybrids.

Or else they're real vampires, and we're epically screwed.

I settle my skipping heartbeat with a low growl. They're blocking the way out. We need to keep this group occupied long enough for Trajan to get somewhere safe, we need Marcus to get back here in one piece, and we need to get the hell out of here.

And if we cull a few of Jacques' allies, that's okay too.

All right then. I glance at each of the wolves next to me. Abby's wolf's calm determination gives me a hit of confidence. Cliffe's wolf vibrates with excitement. *Good*. This kid wants a fight.

Together we move in their direction. The hawk takes off, swooping overhead. A cat yowls, the sound lifting the hairs on my neck. Abby's on my left, matching my pace, while Cliffe lopes easily at my right. The hawk dives at us, a feathered bullet. We scatter and it pulls up, talons extended. Too close.

I start to run, heading for the guy in the middle. He pulls out a pistol. A streak of pain buzzes across my shoulder. I launch myself at him.

I lock my jaws on the wrist of his gun hand, shaking hard. A cat screeches, followed by a sharp bark. I recognize Abby, which sparks anger. The guy I'm fighting yells, "Kill the wolves. Kill all the wolves." I lunge again, this time knocking him to the ground.

A sharp swipe of one paw opens his throat, although he doesn't bleed much. Still, even a strigoi gets slowed down by a wound like that. I check on Cliffe; she's holding her own against a pair of cats. There's already one in the dirt and it's not moving.

Abby's been trapped up against a pile of rocks by a pair of strigoi and a mangy looking wolf. I want to help but the bear picks me as a target. I'm faster—I think—but I won't leave Abby and

Cliffe. So, stand and fight against a creature that's probably double my weight with longer claws. Good times.

I growl, baring my fangs. It's on.

The bear's fast, but I'm faster. The bear is mean, swiping at me with those giant paws.

But god help me, I'm meaner. I clamp my jaw on the meat of one shoulder. He roars, standing up on his hind legs. I hang on, scrabbling my claws against his side.

The hawk shrieks and I catch a flash of movement. On instinct I let go and the bird plows into the bear's thick side. I'm coiling for another spring when a gunshot stops me.

"Desist."

A vampire stands on a rise between us and the road out. He's aiming a pistol into the air and his grin turns my stomach. Cliffe's standing on three paws, snarling silently, and Abby?

Abby's pinned on the ground by a pair of the strigoi. One holds a gun, and it's pointed directly at her head.

"I have so many questions," the vampire says. "So why don't you all get human so you can answer them."

It's not a question. He doesn't say please. I catch Cliffe's eye and give her a nod. She scowls like she's going to protest, so I keep her locked in my glare. After a heartbeat, she bows her head.

I shift, too fucking worried to notice how easy it is. Standing there as naked as the day the doctor slapped my ass, I turn my glare on the vampire. "Tell your friends to lose the gun."

He's tall and slender, with the long curls and sleepy eyes of a romantic poet. *Names probably Raphael or Percy or something*. Flipping a curl over his shoulder, he gives me what's supposed to be a seductive smile. I let my flat expression say I'm not seduced.

He shrugs in a can't-fault-a-guy-for-trying way. "You ignored the signs. No one is supposed to be on this beach at night."

"The signs?" I smirk. "You get 'em from a movie set or something?"

"I have a permit." He tries to out-smirk me, which makes me laugh. I mean, my goal was to give Trajan time to get as far away as possible. Cracking lame jokes works as well as anything else.

"The gun?" I prompt, and Percy waves a hand in Abby's direction. The strigoi ease off, and in a flash of light and heat, Abby shifts. We share a glance and move closer together. Cliffe stretches and flexes one hand, working out the kinks from her wolf's injury.

Percy-the-vampire palms a cell phone. "Now since I did you a favor, you can do one for me.

Tell me who you are and what you're doing here at this time of night."

"I'm David, this is my sister Abby and our friend Cliffe."

"Hmm." He gives us each a once-over. If he thinks he's going to embarrass naked wolves with his wanton gaze, he hasn't spent much time with wolves. His cell phone rings, and though he murmurs, I can hear him pretty easily.

"Yeah, one of them says his name is David." His gaze on me sharpens. "David Collins?" he asks louder.

Fuck. "Yeah."

Another murmur, and my heart turns to stone. Whoever he's talking to has said to bring me…somewhere, and to kill the others.

Nope. Not going to happen. "To me." I give a sharp command. Abby and Cliffe respond before anyone else does. They crowd close. I clasp hands with both of them.

"What'd you…? Don't be like that." Percy pockets the phone. "Somebody get rid of the girls. Jacques only wants David."

"There's not an alpha in the world that'll let you kill his packmates while he still lives. We all go or none of us do."

Percy looks more irritated than anything else. "You're going to fight me with your nasty human hand paws?"

Releasing Abby and Cliffe, I shift. It hurts like fuck, but the stink of scared vampire distracts me. None of the other shifters can take their animal form so soon. Even the hawk is back to being a scrawny dude with a beaky nose. I growl, low, letting my wolf take charge.

"O-kay." The one in charge waves at Abby and Cliffe. "Shoot them now."

I lunge at him, aiming for his 'nads. Abby and Cliffe take off, heading in different directions. Percy leaps away with vampire speed, so I run down the only strigoi who takes off after my pack.

"Stop him!" A gun goes off. Something punches me in the chest, a firebolt that knocks the breath out of me.

"Jesus, you were supposed to shoot him in the ass or something." It's probably the vampire, but the world has gone fuzzy. I'm on my belly in the sand.

"David." Abby screams from very far away. Someone touches me, fingers digging into my fur. "Shift." The hands shake me, making my chest hurt worse. "Shift so you can heal."

It's hard to breathe, harder to think. My wolf has no intention of letting go.

"Come on." She smacks my muzzle. *Abby. Only she'd…*

"Shift!" The word is a scream and a sob.

My wolf howls, although the sound that escapes is more of a tired gurgle. Another pair of hands touch me. Pack. Calling me. Holding me. For the briefest moment, I picture letting go. The promise of peace is enticing, but…

Nah.

I draw another breath, my chest burning with effort. Nudging my wolf out of the way—gratefully, respectfully, but firmly—I shift to my human form.

Shifting might heal the wound in my chest, but every other molecule in my body is screaming.

Someone stands over me, someone wearing a pair of Italian leather loafers that probably cost $800, so it must be Percy. I inhale salt air. Pack surrounds me, warm hands on my bare skin.

"I'm just going to bring them all." The nasal voice is sharp with either irritation or fear, and I'd laugh if I could. *I should be annoyed. I'm the one who got shot, asshole.*

"Look, he wasn't supposed to be able to shift a second time. Lord knows what else he'll do. If you want this David Collins person, you're getting his friends, too."

I've got one eye open but it's too dark to see much. "Come on," Abby says, tugging gently on my shoulders. "Sit up."

It hurts, but I manage to sit. Abby's got an arm around my shoulders and Cliffe is supporting me from the other side. My body is one big bruise, but I manage a glare for Percy. "All or none, boss."

He purses his lips, fists on his hips like he's posing for the cover of *How-to-Homo Magazine*. "If it's not too much trouble, you *all* can follow us to the car."

Snapping his fingers at a couple of strigoi, he pirouettes and stalks off in the direction of the beach road. Abby and Cliffe work together to hoist me up. I'd feel better if I had some meat, raw or cooked, but it's probably too much to ask if we can stop at In-N-Out Burger.

For my first time playing alpha, I fucked up in pretty spectacular fashion. If I pay attention, though, I might learn something useful.

As long as we get out of this alive.

CHAPTER TWENTY-SEVEN

CONNOR

Get here now.

The text from Brodie is unusually terse. I snap to attention, crouched behind a clump of cactus on the bluff overlooking Betancourt's Malibu hideout. Brodie and Sheena are watching the front of the house for any activity, and I have the back. Ninety minutes ago, two oversized SUVs—probably Escalades, since we were dealing with vampires—had headed down the hill at faster-than-legal speed. About three minutes ago two sets of headlights had come back.

My best guess is there's something—or someone—in that car he wants me to see. I make that guess while jogging along the crest of the bluff.

I find Brodie under the rock ledge where I left him, fiddling with his phone. "What?" I pin him with the question, my voice low.

"Look." He passes me the phone.

It's a grainy picture of the Malibu house. Several people are between the SUV and the front door. One of them has familiar bleached-blond hair. Recognition stabs me in the gut. "What the hell?" I whisper.

"I didn't get a great look at any of them, but figured you'd want to know."

I touch the screen to enlarge the photo. Definitely David. He's naked and he's got an arm around Abby. Cliffe walks behind him and a little to his left, the way a lieutenant should. "Oh my fucking god."

Auras don't photograph, but their body language says a lot. Tossing Brodie his phone, I reach for my own, swiping a familiar number even though it's hopeless. When a gruff voice answers, I almost drop it.

"Who's this?"

"Connor? It's me. Marcus."

"What in the hell is going on?"

"David's…in trouble."

"I know that." I force myself to inhale before I start spouting some clichéd gangster dialogue. "Where are you?"

"In the parking lot at the beach. We found the Princess, but some guys stopped us. Trajan took off and I followed him. When I came back, they were marching David and Abby to their cars. I wanted to try and stop them but…"

But what, you chicken shit piece of crap? My jaw's clenched so tight I almost bust a tooth. "I guess if David and Abby together couldn't fight their way free, it wouldn't have done you much good to—"

"I should have done it anyway. I fucked up. Again."

I raise a hand to stop him like he's going to see me through the phone. "Look, I want to hear every damned detail. I'll text you where to be, and you either meet us there in an hour or text me frequent updates letting me know why you're late. If you don't show, asshole, I swear you'll think Randolph Collins let you off light."

Marcus hangs up and I sit gulping air. There are too many gaps for me to make sense out of any of this. "What time is it?"

"Three-thirty."

Okay, so Tray's got a couple hours to get under cover. If he's up in the hills somewhere he'll be able to go to ground. He's been alive too damned long not to. I tick through my reasoning again, setting my expectations. "Where's Sheena?"

"I just messaged her. She'll meet us at the car."

"There's too many of them in there for us to…" I let the idea fade.

Brodie just looks at me and after a minute he shakes his head. "We need more firepower. We didn't come armed for war."

I rake both hands through my hair. I don't want to leave David, but we need more—more information, more allies, more weapons—before we try and bust him out. "We should have told him to meet us here."

"If by *him* you mean the guy we're supposed to text an address to, there's still time to change your mind."

"Good point." Staring in the direction of the house, I play different scenarios in my head. "There's a Duke's down where the canyon road hits the Pacific Coast Highway. Tell him we'll meet him in the parking lot."

"Do you have his phone number?"

"Text David's phone."

"Um, can you give me that number?"

I glare at Brodie, although it's myself I'm angry with. "Yeah. Sorry." I shoot him David's contact information, making a deliberate choice to ignore the leer that crosses Brodie's face.

After a minute he says, "All done."

"He better respond before we get to the car."

Brodie stretches up from his crouch, phone still in his hand. "I'll tell him that, too. We ready to go?"

When Brodie's acting the grown-up, shit's bad. He scrambles down the hill and I follow. Sheena meets us at the car. By the time we're buckled in, Marcus has promised to meet us at Duke's and Sheena's registered her displeasure. Or torn me a new asshole. One of them.

"How many people do you guess Jacques has with him right now?" I manage an adult-adjacent tone of voice and put the car in gear.

Sheena's in the passenger seat, glaring a hole through the front window. "I counted at least forty."

"Sounds about right," Brodie says, from the rear seat. He's sprawled at an angle that won't allow a seat belt to buckle. Whatever. He's part djinn. If we get in a wreck, he'll bounce.

"Three of us against forty-ish opponents of unknown type, with an unknown number of weapons. We don't have a floorplan for the house, so we'll be going in entirely blind. I can think of many outcomes for this situation, but none of them are good."

Sheena grunts, which I take as permission to leave.

Las Flores Canyon Road is dark and winding. Keeping us on the road gives me something to think about besides what's happening to David. If Jacques was going to kill him, they wouldn't have brought him back to the house. He'd be dead. Abby was there, too, and so was Cliffe. He's not alone.

Hoping I'm not delusional, I steer us across the Pacific Coast Highway and into the Duke's parking lot. At this time of night, it's mostly a big stretch of darkness except for a couple pools of light from the streetlights. The ocean sounds close enough to touch. We wait five, maybe ten minutes, until a car takes a right off the highway and pulls up next to us.

Marcus is at the wheel. He's not a lot bigger than David, but he's got broader shoulders, more like Randolph Collins. If he didn't look so starved, I'd think he got the family's husky genes. He's got a baseball cap pulled low, as if the brim will hide the ugly scar where one eye used to be.

Whatever else happened, he's lost his eye patch. Not good.

He gets in the back seat, next to Brodie. "Tell us what happened," I say. I'm not friendly, but then part of me wants to take the guy's dick off, for a couple different reasons, so he can deal.

"They got David, Abby, and your other friend."

"Who's they?" Brodie asks.

Marcus just shakes his head. "We went down to the beach. There were some No Trespassing signs, but…we did it anyway. David, Abby, and Trajan went into the cave and left me and Cliffe keeping watch. While they were gone, a bunch of guys showed up, so we hid behind the pyre."

His voice isn't steady and really, he's kind of pathetic. David once said they'd been best friends, so I reach across and put my hand on his knee. "No judgment, okay. You're not at fault here."

The kid shrugs, his aura a sad grey thing. He's wearing a pair of baggy shorts and was probably lucky to have found those. "When David and the others came out of the cave, Trajan was carrying someone, the Princess, I guess. The guys saw them before we could tell them to hide. David had us shift, and when Trajan took off with the Princess, one of the guys followed him.

"The vampire was fast as fuck, and after a while I lost him entirely. I took care of the other guy, and made sure no one else had followed, then went back to the beach. They were making David and Abby get into one of their SUVs. I wanted to stop them, but we were pretty badly outnumbered."

"So you just watched them go?" He flinched, and I smacked myself for kicking a dog when he was down. "Probably a good thing. Either you'd be dead or you'd be with them, and at least now we've got information that we wouldn't otherwise have."

He nods, and if his expression isn't hopeful, at least it's not quite so bleak. Sheena gives me a "what's next" head tilt and I shake the hair out of my face like that'll somehow give me an answer.

Brodie leans back in the seat, stretching his legs. "Tonight's the big bad, right?"

"According to the witch, it is," I say. "If Trajan's really got the Princess's body, maybe we can work a trade for David." I'd trade places with David in a heartbeat, whether we have the Princess or not. "I'm just not sure I can stand to wait till Trajan gets back."

"I get that, man, but we might not have a choice. Besides, there were a bunch of night crawlers in that house with Jacques. They won't make trouble for David during the day."

I almost don't recognize this new and sympathetic Brodie. "I hope not. I sure as hell hope not."

"We put out a call." Sheena's already got her phone in her hand. "Everyone we can think of who might help. We meet as soon as the sun sets tonight, and we come up with a plan."

"Yeah." I turn the engine on. "That's smart. We'll get David tonight."

I hope.

CHAPTER TWENTY-EIGHT

Being naked doesn't bother me. I mean, I'd rather be dressed to impress in a sick pair of painted-on jeans, but that's not how the night is going.

If I had to prioritize, I'd take food over clothing. Back-to-back shifting has sapped me, but this is no time to get the fades. Abby's got a tight grip on one hand and Cliffe has the other, and so help me I need them both to stay upright. Three carrion-scented zombies keep us moving, their shoving hands slimy and cold.

The house reminds me of Jacques' place in Beverly Hills where we'd camped for a few months: oversized, polished, and soulless. With Percy-the-priss leading the way, we come through the main entrance and into a grand room. The western wall is glass, with a panoramic view of the mountains tumbling down to the ocean. There's no hint of sunrise, which is too bad, because Jacques Betancourt sits opposite us, in the kind of gold throne Trump would envy.

"Mr. Collins, I welcome you and your compatriots."

The three of us stop when P-t-p hisses. "I apologize, Jacques. He refused to leave the women."

A swarm of supernaturals have staked out territory along the perimeter of the room. The place stinks of shifter, with bear and wolf dominating, but there are others. I don't have time to tease out more than a handful, what with the master vampire and his scion dominating my view.

"That's fine, Domingo. I'm sure we'll make use of them."

Jacques' smile makes it plain that *making use of them* could involve throwing Abby and Cliffe to the wolves—literally. Percy's real name is apparently Domingo. Huh. File that bit of info for later, so I can tell Trajan about him.

When I see Trajan again.

Which'll be after the three of us get out of this little clusterfuck.

"Ahem." Jacques draws my wayward attention. "Would you care to explain why you were on that particular beach on this particular night?"

"It's a public beach. Maybe you could tell us why we shouldn't have been there."

He waves away my attitude, his wasted hand as bony and grey as a death claw. "I have a permit."

I can't help laughing. "You want me to believe that you, master vampire, took the time to go to the city website and fill in an application?"

The dead guy behind me smacks my head hard enough to make my ears ring, but Jacques' expression doesn't change.

"Domingo did it for me," he says, his words cut off by a wracking cough.

"Apologies, then. We should have left when Domingo"—I lay on another helping of sarcasm—"showed us the permit. Oh wait."

Abby's grip is tightening, cutting off the circulation to my fingers. I'll have to explain my strategy of antagonism later.

"We couldn't leave when we saw the permit, because Percy's friends got all up in our stuff."

"So it's our fault." Jacques' tone is dry.

Percy starts spouting some manner of self-defense, all but stamping his wittle foot. I keep my gaze on Jacques, who really does look like an animated skeleton. His grey silk suit might have come from Armani, but it hangs on him like a shroud.

"Look, Mr. Betancourt. *Sir.*" I must overshoot the snark because Cliffe tries to turn a laugh into a cough. "Since everything is all nice and legal, we should probably just head out and let you enjoy your"—I glance around the room—"party."

Orgy is more like it. Orgy of supernatural losers. There are even a couple of elves lounging glamour-free near the window, which makes me wonder how much loyalty the Princess really has.

I shift my weight like I'm going to pivot but slimy dead hands grab me. Abby gasps, which is the only warning I have before someone clocks me from behind. I hit my knees, trying not to puke. Abby growls, and I'm vaguely aware of a scuffle around me. Mostly I'm occupied with the throb of pain that comes with each heartbeat.

What'd they hit me with? A baseball bat?

"Stop." Cliffe's cry drags me out of my own head. One zombie dude has her pinned and the other looks ready to tear out her throat with his teeth.

"Hey," I holler, but the sound is weak. Abby shakes off an overweight bear shifter and launches herself in Cliffe's direction. I manage to drag my way to my feet, despite the way my head is spinning. We're surrounded, catching fists and claws faster than we can fight them off.

They're going to tear us to pieces. I play the only card I have left.

"Jacques Betancourt, if you kill the children of the American Alpha and their packmate, your life will be forfeit."

No way he could hear me over the noise. A couple dead guys are gripping my arms with slimy determination, ignoring my attempts to shake them off.

Some must have heard me, though, because there's a break in the action. A quick glance tells me the wolves in the room have paused.

"Desist." Jacques' command carries a lot more weight, and even more of the supernatural hooligans subside. The three of us are pinned in place, but at least no one's actively trying to kill us.

Jacques stands, but it's a slow process. A woman slips out of the crowd and comes to his side. She's pretty—if you like your sweeties surgically enhanced—and he drapes a possessive arm around her shoulders.

"You think your father would avenge a pervert like you?" He moves in my direction, his steps unsteady.

"He would," Abby says, her voice clear and strong. One of the zombies shakes her as if that'll shut her up. Her low and threatening growl shows how well that worked.

His leer is trying to undermine my confidence. That's not working, either. The only way to deal with someone as powerful as Jacques Betancourt is to meet them with confidence. "I mean, are you really willing to take that chance? Dad's not known for his patience with idiots."

Jacques' gaze narrows, the only thing giving his face life. "Maybe I am willing to take that chance."

"And maybe I think we're more use to you alive than dead."

"How so?"

"Because there's a piece you're missing." My grin is way cockier than I feel.

"Tell me."

I shrug. "Let go of my sister and my packmate and maybe I will."

Jacques waves a hand at Percy, who's sidled away from the fighting so he won't get his Salvador Ferragamos dirty. Percy's eyes get real wide, as if Jacques just yelled in his head the way he's been yelling in Trajan's. Percy marches over to Cliffe, producing a nasty-looking blade from his jacket's inner pocket.

"This one?" Percy lays the blade flat against Cliffe's throat and Jacques laughs.

"It doesn't matter. Now"—he turns to me—"are you persuaded to tell me this vital piece of information?"

I start laughing, because *shit, man*. I'm standing naked in front of a room full of wanna-bes and the only thing between the three of us and a gory death is my ability to entertain this twisted old demon. I reach for my wolf, tapping into the source of whatever power I've been granted, and raise one hand. "Wolves, down."

Across the room, a dozen or so men and women drop to their knees. A quick scan shows me the only other wolves in the room are Abby and Cliffe. It also shows me that my innards are fixing to bust with the effort this is costing me. "Wolves, move."

Okay, the last word is more of a gasp, but I fill the space with my intention. One by one, every wolf in the place turns toward Jacques. "If I tell them to kill," I manage to grind out, "they're coming for you."

His eyes are flaming pits. "Take them to the waiting room." He's swaying on his feet, despite the help of his plastic girlfriend. "I must give this matter more thought."

His tone says he's not backing down, that this is a strategic retreat. I know better. I let go of my hold on the room, a little nervous the wolves will retaliate. Percy's back before that can happen, directing our zombie friends—and us—down a hall and into what has to be the smallest room in the house.

The only piece of furniture is a bunk that looks older than anyone here except maybe Jacques, and for a small space, the stink of fear and desperation is impressive. Nothing good has ever happened here. Abby, Cliffe, and I are shoved through the door and a sharp click says it's locked behind us.

Good. If we're locked in, they're locked out. "We've bought ourselves some time," I say, flopping against a wall and sliding down to my butt. "Let's see what we can come up with."

Cliffe claims the bunk and Abby stakes out a section of the floor, but before they can answer me, a sharp scream tears through the air.

"You've lost her, you idiot."

A stream of protest is cut off by a dense grunt, then silence.

"Clean this up."

More silence. We glance at each other, their uncertainty echoing mine. Best case, Jacques now knows Trajan took off with the Princess's body and had Percy staked as punishment.

Worst case? I decide I don't want to ponder the worst case scenarios, in case the universe wants to take me up on one.

CHAPTER TWENTY-NINE

TRAJAN

Waiting until sunset is the hardest thing I've ever done. Well, the second-hardest, after leaving David and Abby on the beach with Jacques' allies. I'd seen at a glance that they were strigoi and shifters. David's exceptionally capable, but…

I shrink back into the nest I've made, willing the sun to set. I'm between a pile of rocks and a large cluster of rhododendrons, their leathery leaves blocking most of the light. My skin prickles in spots where the shade is thin, but I'm safe enough.

The Princess Tatiana lies beside me, cool and unmoving. Even without her glamour, I recognized the shape of her eyes and her soft brown curls. If Jacques needs her body to work his spell, I have no idea what he'll do when he finds her missing.

But it won't be good.

Sending my senses out, I search for anyone who might have followed us. Nothing. I brush against the small creatures that live in the mountains, none of them dangerous. I'd rested for a brief while, and now have nothing to do but wait.

The sound of her voice makes me jump. Fortunately the sun is low in the sky, so I don't fry.

"His rage is a poison."

The Princess's body hasn't moved. I'm not honestly sure I heard the words or if she's somehow spoken right into my head. "Has he discovered that you're missing?"

"He killed the one who let you go."

Let me go? "I thought I escaped all on my own."

"Poison. He's poison. He'll kill anyone who crosses him. You must not let him win."

"I don't intend to."

"The cost to you will be high, maybe too high, but you must defeat him."

Through all of this her body hasn't moved. I'm not sure who I'm talking to, or if we're talking at all. Maybe I'm overtaxed, overtired, making shit up for my own entertainment. "And if I'm not successful?"

"Your lovers will die, and you will face endless torment. The immense power Jacques desires will cost every vampire, for the elves will avenge me in the most brutal way possible."

Okay, so that's pretty convincing. "I'll do what I can."

Her shriek almost sends me out into the dying sunlight. "Okay, I won't let him win."

"Swear it."

"I…swear." I must not satisfy her, because she shrieks again.

"Swear it in blood."

I don't have a pocketknife or anything like it, so I slice the palm of my hand with my thumbnail. A trickle of blood drips slowly from the wound. "I swear to you I will defeat Jacques Betancourt and do what I can to reunite your spirit with your body."

She doesn't answer, but that's okay. The sun has dropped low enough to cast the mountains in shadow. Before I stand, I send my senses out a second time. This time I'm looking for Connor and David.

I only find Connor. Dread pools in my belly. *I should never have left him on the beach.* Orienting myself to Connor's presence, I pick up the Princess's body and start to run.

I stand in front of that same Motel 6, still carrying the Princess. The evening commute goes on around me. If anyone thinks a homeless-adjacent guy with an unconscious woman in his arms is a strange sight, they keep it to themselves.

LA, man. LA.

I don't want to test their tolerance by walking through the lobby. Instead, I pull the shadows around me and my burden. I stop just inside, casting around for the stairs. There. A door, next to the elevators. I take them two at a time, climbing the six flights to our room. When I get there, I can't knock with the Princess in my arms, and it would be rude to walk in unannounced. I simply call his name.

"Connor."

The door pops open like he's been waiting right inside. "*Dia á sábháil*. You're here."

Our gazes lock, a jumble of words we can't say. He flicks a glance at the Princess, then steps aside so I can enter.

Brodie, the one from the Elites, is stretched out on one bed, and Sheena's in the chair. Brodie gives me a sleepy grin and closes his eyes, as if he thinks we'll have privacy if he isn't looking.

"David." Connor's husky cry pulls my attention back to him.

"Where is he? I can't find him."

Connor's expression tightens and he stares across the room. "In the house. Jacques' house in Malibu."

The dread I'd been running from now weighs down my limbs. The Princess is unbearably heavy, and moving slowly so neither of us shatter, I set her down on the other bed. "I left him on the beach. He had…others, and I needed to get the Princess away. It's…my fault. I shouldn't have left him."

"I left him too," a new voice says.

I spin in his direction, tensed for a fight. Marcus is looking as shabby as I am.

"When you took off, one of them followed you." Marcus grimaces. "David told me to go after him, so I did."

I hadn't sensed any pursuit. "You kill him?"

Marcus shrugged. "Yeah."

"Thanks."

"There were too many of them, though, and…"

Connor picked up when Marcus's words faded. "Early this morning, we saw David, Abby, and Cliffe get marched into Jacques' house."

I collapse on the edge of the bed, hands covering my face. "Okay, so how do we get him out?"

"We don't." Connor hands me a folded piece of paper. Jacques' familiar calligraphy makes a bad situation so much worse.

You have something I want, and I have something you want. I suggest a trade. Your minions have already scouted the location, and if necessary, I can perform the spell with a werewolf sacrifice. I suggest you arrive well before midnight.
J.

"I have a plan." Connor crouches next to me, his hands on my knees. "*Mo shíorghrá*, we can save him."

"But the Princess…"

"We just needed to be sure you had her." He doesn't let go of me, shifting his weight so he's sitting on his heels. "Are you satisfied, *onóir amháin?*"

I straighten, covering Connor's hands with my own. A woman materializes, a crone. The Morrigan.

"We have a bargain, *meascach*." She stands behind the couch, absently toying with one of Brodie's blond dreads. He doesn't seem to mind, but Marcus eases away from all of us. "I'll create an identical copy of the body for you to offer in trade."

"How long?" Connor sounds reluctant.

"Give me the real Princess."

My gaze narrows. "That doesn't answer his question."

She laughs, an unhinged sound. "Give me the Princess and I'll have the replica ready in an instant."

Connor and I share a glance. His skepticism echoes my own, but I don't see that we have a choice. We both stand and the Morrigan passes close enough for me to catch the scent of something raw and moist. She reaches the Princess and, without another word, she vanishes.

So does the Princess.

"Fuck." The word lurches out.

"That," Connor finishes for me.

Brodie just laughs. "Mack, you have the strangest assortment of friends and acquaintances I've ever come across."

Connor shakes his head, massaging his neck with one hand. "Shut up, djinn."

"So, what now?" I ask. The Morrigan's stink hasn't faded and it makes me feel unclean. "I could use a shower."

"Yeah, man. Get cleaned up. I'll rally the troops. We're meeting in Stone's conference room in an hour."

Connor's businesslike tone calms me. "Troops?"

He gives me a sad smile. "Every damned person I know in the city of Los Angeles, plus a few I haven't yet met."

I glance at Sheena and she gives me a sharp nod. That reassures me even more. "All right, then. Let's do this."

By the time I'm done with my shower and have slicked my hair out of my face, Connor has set things in motion. "From Stone's, we'll go to the target location."

Brodie's laughter cuts him off. "And then we'll raise hell, my dudes."

"I might just like this guy," Sheena says, giving Brodie side-eye.

Connor's eye roll is subtle, but it still makes me smile. He tilts his head toward the bed where I first set the Princess. She — or rather an exact copy of her body — is just where I left her. "Sometimes having a living god in your family tree comes in handy."

We're staring at each other again, and the others fade out of my awareness. "We must get David out of this alive."

He nods so earnestly I wonder if this is the first time I've seen the real, honest Connor MacPherson.

"We must also destroy Jacques Betancourt before he can carry out his spell," he murmurs.

But Jacques' destruction won't mean shit if David doesn't survive. I keep that thought to myself, though, and clasp Connor's hand. "We'll do this, *amore mio*. We must succeed."

PART FOUR: BINDING COPPER, GOLD, & MOONLIGHT

CHAPTER THIRTY

DAVID

I shake out the trousers, the legs clown-wide and the waistband riding low on my hips. About eight sizes too large, they smell like cigarettes and blood. I don't want to think too hard about the scabby flecks of…something scattered over the fabric.

Tearing a couple strips off an old tee shirt, I use one as a belt and the other as a bandage. When I'd asked nicely for some clothes, the scum sucker they'd left in charge had gotten mouthy. I argued the point, and it took three of them to drag me off him.

They did toss us some clothes, so maybe that means I won. I don't know. In addition to the ongoing ringing in my head from this morning's baseball bat, my right eye's swollen shut and my ribs are bruised. If I end up with a scar, those fuckers'll be sorry.

We're still locked in the tiny room of grief, and Abby and Cliffe dig through the pile. Cliffe pulls on a pair of shorts and an oversized tee, and Abby finds some jeans.

The best she can find for a top is a man's white button-down with a dark red splatch of gore on one side of the collar. Before she puts the shirt on, she rips the collar off, her expression blank.

"This must be where they stash their next meals. Anybody got a cigarette?" Cliffe asks. *Oh fuck. She had to say cigarette.*

"You don't smoke." *And I don't smoke either. Ahhh…*

She shrugs and settles onto the antique bunk. The thing squeals in protest. "Supposed to give a prisoner one last meal, but since so many of these fuckers drink blood…"

"Last meal," I scoff, dropping onto "my" patch of floor. "What kind of talk is that? Do you think we need a last meal?" I aim the question at Abby.

She's standing against the wall, and before she answers, she slides down so she's squatting with her elbows resting on her knees. "Nah," she says, interlacing her fingers. "My last meal's going to be better than anything these asswipes can come up with."

"Asswipes." I snicker, but yeah, that's my sister. Collins is shorthand for confidence.

Cliffe groans and stretches out on the bunk. "You two. You seriously think…nah, never mind." She covers her face with her hands, as if she hopes we won't see her fear. I can smell it, though, cutting through the funk of blood and smoke and desperation.

"Yes, I do think." I say it quietly, giving the words time to sink in. "I mean, they're not going to unlock the door and tell us there's an Uber out front, but as soon as we see a chance, we're going to take it."

"And do what?" Cliffe's words are muffled by her hands.

"Run," Abby says with a small smile. We're both pint-sized, but she's got Mom's soft features. She's got Dad's dark eyes, too, and it's the daughter of the American Alpha who's watching Cliffe carefully.

Cliffe sits up, shaking lank hair in front of her face. "Maybe one of his boyfriends will rescue us."

"Or maybe we'll rescue ourselves." I speak firmly. God knows what good it'll do, but if we don't believe we can get out of this, we might as well give up. "Here's what I think." I tap on the floor, making up a plan on the fly. "They must want us for a reason, or we'd be dead."

"True."

Abby's assurance reinforces my own. "Regardless of what happens next, we all need to stay alert, and if any of us see a break, an opportunity, a…shit, I don't know, anything like an opening, holler and we'll all run." Okay, it's not much of a plan, but it's better than diving into a collective well of despair.

"What should we holler?" Cliffe might not actually buy what I'm selling, but her snarky tone is a step in the right direction.

"Pork belly." My mouth might be smirking, but my gaze is steady. "Anyone who sees an out yells "pork belly" and we all take off."

Abby rocks forward and smacks me on the arm. "You don't even like pork."

"Now that I think about it, I could really use some beef."

She raises both hands. "I do not want to know, brother of mine. You keep your salacious details to yourself."

I snicker, but Cliffe has gone rigid.

"The copper heart has the most to lose, and all hinges on his choice."

Her voice sounds as if three people are talking at once, and one of them's being tortured. Abby and I share a glance. "Uh, what?"

Cliffe blinks like she's just taken a thirty-second nap. "I don't know. What?"

Abby's on the alert. "You just said something about a copper heart."

With a shrug, Cliffe slumps against the wall. "Psychic, my dudes. My other sense has a shitty sense of timing."

"That's so cool, though." Abby's grin is the brightest thing in the place. "I mean, the ability to spout semi-meaningful nonsense in critical situations is something we should all cultivate."

I raise my eyebrow at her. "You've been spending too much time with our mother."

"Mom would l-o-v-e Cliffe."

Cliffe laughs, her cheeks so pink she must be embarrassed. Abby's not wrong, though. "I look forward to bringing you home to meet Mom."

Just as soon as we get out of here.

CHAPTER THIRTY-ONE

CONNOR

Stone's conference room table seats eight, but we have more than that present. In addition to me, Trajan, and Stone, there's Lydia and her girl Accalia, Sheena, the magician Albion Bird, David's cousin Marcus, and Sam Kowalski.

Stone volunteers to stand in the doorway so the rest of us can have a seat. His aura is solid, secure, a dark mix of colors that boost my confidence. I turn to him when the mix of auras at the table gets too agitated for me to sort one from the other. Reading the room, I see nervous energy verging on fear. Even Trajan's clear blue is spiked with red and grey.

Anger and sadness.

We need to retrieve David.

I don't want to start with something as banal as *Thank you all for coming*, but I am grateful. "So here's the deal. Sometime between now and midnight, Jacques Betancourt is going to try to siphon off Princess Tatiana's life force to reinforce his own."

"How?" Stone asks, a legit question.

Marcus surprises me by speaking up first. "He's built a pyre and he's going to burn her body. We gotta get David and Abby out before he does."

That prompts a confusing round of chatter from everyone present, one that doesn't end until Stone speaks up again. "No, I mean how is he doing it? Dude's been a vampire a long time, but this shit's next level."

Trajan's gone sheet white, his unruly hair blocking my view of his eyes. "He had them staked," he says. He's staring at his phone and when he straightens, all I see is horror.

Horror that echoes the rising terror in my heart. "Who?"

"He had Gillian and Peter staked."

"Oh." I sag with relief. If he'd staked David…

Trajan covers his face with his hands. "I gave him undeath, and now he's gone. They're both gone."

Sheena's sitting at Trajan's side across the table from me. She wraps an arm around his shoulders, and when he looks up a second time, his aura is the bright orange of a caution sign. Anger verging on rage. "He cannot be allowed to live."

Sheena's arm becomes less about comfort and more about restraint.

I stand, intending to take charge before things get even more out of control. "The short answer is," I say, speaking loud to cut through the noise, "we don't know how he's doing it. He's tapping some unknown resources and he's probably been doing so for a while. For years."

"Warlock." Albion Bird speaks into the relative silence. "He has a warlock on his side, for sure."

"Yes, and apparently that warlock has created a legion of strigoi." I've got their attention now. Lydia's expression is grim. Sheena looks thunderous. "But we've got the Princess's body, so there's that."

"What?" The elf leaps to his feet. "Why are we wasting time here, then? Give her to me. You must give her to me now."

I look Kowalski straight in the eye. "No."

He bursts into a storm of words, speaking in a language I don't understand. Trajan stands, though, and snaps a finger in front of Kowalski's face. The elf turns to Trajan, drawing a breath for more invective, and Trajan's got him. They lock gazes and the vampire raises a finger.

Kowalski goes silent. Trajan gestures for him to sit, and the elf sits.

"Okay," I say, drawing most everyone's attention away from Trajan's display of control. "We've got the Princess's body, but Jacques has David Collins, his sister Abby, and our new packmate Cliffe."

"Aw shit." Lydia fists her hands, her knuckles going white. "How the hell did that happen?"

"Long story. Jacques has offered to make a trade, though." This is the part that's going to get sticky, at least in terms of the elf. "We give him the Princess's body and he gives us David."

"No!" Kowalski's outrage bursts through Trajan's control. "You will not. No wolf is worth the life of an elven princess. None."

That sets off a firestorm of argument settled only when Stone hollers, "Shut up. All of you shut the fuck up and let him finish."

Everyone quiets down, except for Kowalski, who has a dagger drawn on Sheena. She's got ahold of his wrist, and her grin is the stuff of nightmares.

"Enough." Stone channels his troll half and brings things to a halt. Once he has the room quiet, he nods at me.

In turn, I nod at Kowalski. "We have a replica of the Princess's body. She will not burn, but if you can't control yourself, you can go."

"Replica?" he mutters. "Where did you find a replica?"

"I gave it to him." Ananda Pendragon, the Morrigan, appears next to me at the head of the table. *Shit.*

This apparently causes Kowalski so much outrage he's speechless. Small favors.

"Once we have reunited Tatiana's spirit with her body, she can choose whether to return to her family or stay with me," Ananda Pendragon continues, digging my grave deeper with the elves.

Even from the side, my great-whatever grandmother's smile is pure malice. I shrug her off, trying to get back to the reason we're all here. "We have a replica of the Princess. Now all we need is a plan."

She points at Marcus. "Get up and let an old woman sit."

He does, and I refrain from rolling my eyes.

"I'll carry the Princess's body," Trajan says, "and come back with David."

"You'll need these." Sheena produces a bundle of stakes from under the table.

"I can't walk up to him with a stake in my hand."

"This'll help." Albion Bird sketches a sigil on the tabletop and the stakes fade from sight. "The shade won't last for long, but I'll set it again when we arrive."

Trajan's still red hot, and while I don't blame him, it's not a side of him I've seen before. "I'll carry the Princess, you take the stakes, and we'll do whatever is necessary. Together."

"Together." Trajan meets my gaze and for a few heartbeats, no one else matters. There's trust in his gaze, and a deep connection.

He's it for me. He and David.

We spend a few minutes figuring out who has weapons and who needs them. Brodie says he'll borrow some from Headquarters. He promises Sheena and Stone he'll bring them toys, but he doesn't make the same offer to Kowalski. Elves don't need much more than their nasty attitudes. Albion Bird and the other witches have their own toys. The wolves are most powerful on four legs, I won't need anything more than my pistol, and all Trajan wants is a stake.

"We might be outnumbered," Trajan says, "but we won't be outgunned."

I can't argue with him. "From what we saw, Betancourt has around forty allies, although it's likely he'll be calling in more."

"Why would anyone respond to his call?"

"Power," a new voice says. A vampire stands next to Stone in the doorway. He looks young, although it's impossible to guess his actual age. "He's made some very generous promises to those who will help him."

"Who are you?" I don't mean to sound testy, but it sure comes out that way.

He directs his response to Trajan. "Madame Packard sent me, along with three others. Jacques Betancourt must not be allowed to survive this night."

Trajan retreats into anger, and the four vampires file in.

"Happy to have you along," I say. "Tonight will be a test. We must destroy Betancourt and we must retrieve David and the others. Anyone who doesn't want to face this, say so now."

No one says a word.

"Okay. We'll see you at the beach at ten p.m."

That's about ninety minutes longer than I want to wait, but we need the time to bring in more people and more weapons. And what we lack in numbers, we make up for in commitment.

I hope.

CHAPTER THIRTY-ONE

Trajan

The parking lot is full, and for some reason that makes me laugh. "I mean, is it really a diabolical plot if you don't have a cast of thousands to witness it?"

Connor shakes his head at my sarcasm. He double parks behind a janky-looking SUV and Sheena's headlights flash through our rear window. She's got Marcus, Stone, and Brodie and she's ready to fight.

The witches—there are four of them—are already on the path leading down to the beach. They must have grabbed the last parking spot. Lydia and her girls roar in. Madame Packard's four vampires follow. I don't see the elves—yet— but that might not be a bad thing.

Judging by the number of cars in the lot, we're still badly outnumbered. "That's okay," I murmur. "We'll cut off the head and the rest will scatter."

"That's the plan." Connor pops the lock, ready to rumble. "I'll carry the Princess, and you take on Jacques."

I reach for his hand. "*Amore mio*." Emotion chokes the sound to a whisper.

"We'll bring him home, *mo shíorghrá*. Let's go."

We don't have a plan, per se. The ground rises between the parking lot and the beach and we intend to fan out, keeping within sight of one another and surrounding the action. Now that we're here, a heavy sense of foreboding blots out the sound of the waves and the scent of sea air.

Jacques doesn't just have an advantage in numbers. He's calling up some heavy hitting power, the kind of thing I'd rather avoid.

But he staked my first scion, and he's got David. He will die.

The witches climb to the highest point at the south end of the parking lot, standing in a small circle and facing each other. I jog over, carrying Sheena's stakes with a strap looped around my waist. With a nod, Albion Bird hides them.

Marcus joins Lydia and her wolves, their numbers bolstered by members of two other local packs. Daddy Randolph Collins must not have been amused when he found out both his kids were being detained by a crazed vampire. If he'd had another day or two, he would have sent us an army. There may be others in the shadows, vampires from the viscount or one of the other area sires, but they're unlikely to step in until the winner is clear.

As it is, we number about thirty, maybe thirty-five. Not enough to take on Jacques' crew, but hopefully we won't have to. Hopefully we'll distract Jacques with the fake Princess and get David, Abby, and Cliffe away from him. Then I'm going to do what I must.

Connor comes up behind me, carrying the Princess. We share a glance and at his nod, we head for the beach.

If Jacques has assigned anyone to watch for intruders, we don't see them. We scramble around rocks and tufts of beach grass, using moonlight to navigate. The sky is clear and the steady pulse of the waves undercuts the sound of voices. Many voices. Easily one hundred.

I reach the top of the hill, Connor on one side and Sheena on the other. The smell of gasoline blends with salt and fish and brimstone. The beach is crowded with all manner of supernatural creatures. Shifters, some on four legs, some on two; more of the strigoi we'd dealt with at the house; pixies, coyotes, and at least one troll.

Jacques stands at the center of it all, leaning on the arm of a slight young woman. He gives the impression of weakness, except for the dreadful power pulsing from him.

David is beside him, surrounded by a posse of strigoi. Abby and Cliffe are further away with their own escort. Oddly, the sullen vampire who'd been with Delia Packard stands behind Jacques, his smile as disturbing as anything else in the scene.

Lydia points to Abby and Cliffe and a cadre of wolves move in their direction.

There's a sharp squeal and a flurry of excited laughter. Cliffe stumbles as if someone has smacked her. Before they can cause any more trouble, I holler, "Stop."

My voice carries, amplified by my anger and fear. I stride down the dunes. The attention being directed toward me gives me even more reason to confront the creature who made me as I am.

"Jacques Betancourt, what you are doing here is evil." My words bring a hush over the crowd and I press on. "You are defying the laws of nature, and I intend to stop you."

"You do?" Jacques' laughter is unhinged. The crowd parts so we're standing opposite one another, separated by several hundred feet. "Your argument is lacking. In the first place, you and I break the laws of nature simply by existing, so I hardly see how one little spell does any more damage to your precious laws."

"If it's just a little spell, then you shouldn't need an audience. Send everyone home. Come on, David. Let's leave him to his little spell."

More shattered laughter. "Don't go anywhere, wolf. I've already told Trajan what it will cost to get his lover back." He points at me. "Bring me the Princess's body and he's yours."

Connor steps up beside me. "She's here." Together, we walk toward him, those who have sworn him allegiance crowding around us. Every step is harder than the last one. His power buffets us, stinging like windblown sand.

We stop some ten feet from him. The space between my shoulder blades itches, as if waiting for a knife. I'm holding onto one of the stakes, but loosely, keeping it low. Jacques releases his hold on the woman supporting him and totters in our direction.

"There she is," he says, nothing close to sanity left in his expression. His eyes are unnaturally wide, his cheeks shadowed and sunken. He comes close enough to touch the Princess's arm with clawed and jagged fingernails.

He points at the pyre, the ten-foot pile of wood next to the water. The tide is out, so it'll be a while before the waves reach it. "Take her," he whispers, his smile turning sly. "Take her to the top of the pyre."

Connor and I exchange glances. This wasn't in our playbook, but the wood's not burning yet, so he should be able to leave the Princess's body and make it down. I don't like it, but I don't see a way around it.

Connor turns toward the pyre and again the crowd shifts, giving him a clear view. There don't appear to be stairs, so he'll have to climb up the stacked bundles of wood. Some of the wood glistens in the moonlight, the source of the gasoline smell.

"Be quick," I say, a sense of dread building.

Behind me somewhere, David says "No," the word cut off sharply. The stake grows heavy. If Jacques has done anything to David, I'll…

Connor reaches the pyre and, shifting the Princess to free one hand, starts to climb. For every toehold he finds, he loses two others to the slippery wood. The smell of gasoline grows stronger. I should have carried the Princess. I could have leapt to the top of the pile without climbing. Instead, I'm stuck watching him struggle, and I hate it.

Reaching the top, Connor stands. He settles the Princess in his arms and turns to face us. "She's here, Betancourt. Now let David go."

"Light it."

One cue, three of Jacques' minions toss burning torches at the gasoline-soaked wood.

The pyre bursts into flame like it's been hit by a meteorite.

"Connor!" The word is torn from me, leaving a wound. He stands on the top of the pyre, still holding the Princess, surrounded by smoke and flames. "Jump, you idiot. Leave her there and jump."

He doesn't jump, and with a giant woosh, the pyre is completely engulfed in flame. I'm vaguely aware that David runs toward the fire but someone — probably Sheena — stops him. Jacques' allies are cheering with exultation, and Jacques himself…

Jacques has his eyes on the heavens, his hands raised. He's mouthing words I can't hear. He's so intent on his spell, in fact, that he doesn't see me coming.

This is my chance, my moment. He's threatened everything I value. Still, I hesitate, giving in to one hundred and fifty years of doubt.

Oh, hell no. Never again.

"You bastard," I scream, and for a heartbeat he looks at me, eyebrows raised as if he's confused.

With no hesitation, no question in my mind, I shove the stake into his heart. His confusion turns to shock, his eyes go dark, and then, he's gone. He's too old and powerful to fall into a pile of dust — Buffy Summers had it wrong — so for good measure, I tear off his head.

That look of surprise will stay with me, haunting my moments of uncertainty. So be it. I want to yell at him, to tell him I'm not ashamed of who I am, that I'm man enough to stand up to him.

That I love two men above all else, and he can fuck right off if he thinks I'd give either one of them up.

Instead, I survey the debacle around me, my whole body pulsing with pain. There's fighting, but it's sporadic. The fire burns, but the heat and flames are already fading. Someone comes close, startling me.

The familiar scent of wolf cuts through the nightmare stink of smoke. "David? He's gone."

"No." David's defiance is like a slap in the face. "He'll be back. He will."

I grab hold of his hands, his warmth a touchstone in a sea of despair. "He was standing in the middle of a firebomb, puppy. I don't see how he could have survived."

David doesn't answer, but he doesn't let go of my hands, either. We're interrupted by a trio of strigoi. I lunge at one but he dodges and keeps running. They're being chased by a pair of vampires who make short work of them. It's in the best interest of the other vampire sires to destroy the strigoi Jacques conjured.

Chaos surrounds us, fire and pain and Connor is gone. Brodie and Sheena are tag-teaming a couple of Jacques' scions. Lydia has planted herself in front of Abby and Cliffe, her menacing glare enough to keep the bad guys away. Clusters of shifters on four legs keep up the battle, but many more have run away. Jacques' troll has vanished, or else Stone chased him off, and so has Delia Packard's vampire. Better yet, that horrible sense of evil is fraying like foam whipped off the waves.

I pull David closer. "It's too much to hope that he's faked his own death a second time."

David clenches my shirt in his fists, his face pressed against my chest. "Of course he has. The copper heart has the most to lose, and all hinges on his choice."

"What?"

"Something Cliffe said, back at Jacques' house."

Cliffe. The psychic lesbian werewolf. "She said something to me, too. When we first met." I scramble through my memories. "Something about how he cannot die. I wasn't sure if she meant Jacques or Connor."

David lays his palm on my cheek. "Pretty sure she didn't mean Jacques."

He's right about that. That awareness of my maker, the sense of him I hadn't entirely lost even after I created a scion of my own, is gone. For the first time in one hundred and fifty years, I am alone.

But not entirely.

I rest my cheek on David's head, holding him tight as if I'll be able to absorb his assurance through my skin. Whenever I close my eyes, I see Connor surrounded by flame. I reach out, searching for him on some essential level. I'm not sure what I find. "Do you still feel him?"

David sighs. "The bonds of pack are so thin they'd make a spider's web look sturdy, but he's not gone yet."

Yet?

We're interrupted by Cliffe and Abby. They're holding hands, both of them bruised and dirty. Marcus trails behind, until David holds out an arm and draws all three of them into our little circle of calm.

Sheena comes next, her expression grim. Brodie's right behind her. "Tell me he had an escape route planned," Brodie says, watching the burning pyre.

"No." That's all there is to say.

Sheena holds up a key fob. "He must have figured things would turn out this way because he gave me the key to his rental car to hold onto *just in case.*"

He knew? My head throbs, the swings from hope to despair tightening like a vice around my temples. A distant siren distracts all of us. "Let's go," David says, "before the cops show up."

He's right, but I don't want to leave. "We should wait till the fire burns down a little bit more, in case…"

"Come on." David wraps an arm around my waist, urging me on. "He wouldn't want us to get arrested."

He's not wrong, but I still can't make my feet move.

"It'll be okay, Tray. Let's just get out of here."

Wondering if Connor said something to David that he didn't want me to hear, I give in and follow him over the dunes.

We're chased away by the smell of smoke.

CHAPTER THIRTY-TWO

CONNOR

I'm in a place with no sense of time. I'm awake, aware. No pain. No heat, no chill. My hands are empty.

I am alone.

I start walking because doing something beats sitting there waiting to die. I'm not going to die, or maybe I already have. The ground I'm covering is smooth dirt, nothing to trip over. Yet.

Walking gives me time to remember and time to reflect on those memories. I'd known happiness more than sadness. I'd given pleasure, but I'd also caused pain. I know these things but they're disconnected facts, not tied to specific names and faces.

That is, until two names and two faces come into focus. David, my golden wolf. Trajan, my moonlit soul.

Tiny silver filaments emerge from me and disappear into the distance. So fragile, those ties that hold me to them.

So fragile, and so precious.

I don't know where I'm going and I'd have walked forever if I hadn't heard someone say, "Stop."

Stop.

A single command, the voice familiar. I remember that voice, which causes me to remember other things. Trajan and David, watching the firestorm rage.

I'd been afraid of that, afraid of causing them pain.

That's why I'd insisted on carrying the Princess. Had Trajan carried her up the pyre, he'd be forever dead.

I'm just…somewhere, waiting for a new set of instructions.

"I've lived a long time," the voice says, that same familiar voice. Not my mother, but somehow like her. "And I've seen more things than you could ever imagine."

"I've seen quite a bit," I say, forcing my chin up, my shoulders square.

Laughter, followed by quick running footsteps. "You've got balls, *meascach*. I'll give you that much."

Ananda Pendragon. The Morrigan.

"What have you done, crow?"

She comes close so I can see her. "What have *I* done? I believe the correct question is what have *you* done? *I* gave you a way to fool Betancourt, may his soul burn forever in the pit. You're the one who stayed long enough to cross over."

"Cross over into where?"

"The Netherworld," a new voice says. More footsteps, and the Morrigan is no longer alone. A woman stands at her side, a woman with golden brown curls, pointed ears, and the fierce mouth of an elf.

I bow my head, saluting the Princess Tatiana. "It is good to see you, Princess. I hope you are recovered."

"Well enough. You may be asked to make reparations to Kowalski and his gang, and if so, tell him I said he can eat shit and die. They couldn't control me then, and they can't control me now."

"Good point." I pinch my own leg and twitch when it hurts. "You're assuming I'll make it back to a place where Kowalski can bother me."

The Morrigan cackles. "You can go back any time you like."

"Really? I didn't bring my ruby slippers."

"Come on." She's in her maiden form, her fair skin and dark hair a lovely complement to the Princess. I follow the two of them through the darkness, unsure of where we're going or what we'll see.

I stifle my questions and after a while—like, after the length of time it takes to walk a mile, if I was someplace where time and distance mattered—we approach a door. Or rather, a tall rectangle outlined in warm light. The Morrigan goes through first, then the Princess, and finally, me.

I've only taken a few steps when I stop again. I don't know much about the Netherworld, but we seem to be standing on a small island in the center of a lake. There's nothing on the island besides a kayak, and the black water fades into darkness at the horizon.

Maybe it's not a lake. Maybe my reality has simply narrowed to this small plot of land with about a six-foot diameter and maybe I'm alone.

I'm alone.

While I've been trying to decide where the world ends, the Princess and the Morrigan have disappeared. I kneel down. The ground is damp, as if the water is already working to swallow me up.

"You won't be here long enough for that to happen."

I just about come out of my skin. A man stands behind me. He's old, though I sense his age in the way he carries himself rather than from his physical appearance. My height, same copper hair; *damn, if you told me this dude is my father, I'd believe you.*

"Who are you?"

"I am Arawn, ruler of Annwn." He is wrapped in a long grey cloak with a crown made from antlers. When he quiets, those things fade away and he's an ordinary man in jeans and a sweatshirt.

An ordinary man who looks a lot like me.

His smile has a touch of indulgence. "If I were to tell you that I am your father, what then? Would you want to join me in Annwn, to learn those skills a man should pass on to his son?"

I brush the hair out of my face, a stalling tactic more than anything else. If I say no, will that make him angry?

But if I say yes, will I spend the rest of my life in the Underworld?

Because yeah, Mom taught me enough Celtic mythology for me to understand what he is really saying. "I'd like to believe I already possess the skills that make me a man."

His smile broadens. "You do, Connor MacPherson. You have grown to be the kind of man I'd be proud to call my son."

Unsure whether that was an admission or just a pretty compliment, I push a little more. "My mother never told me anything about my father."

"Your mother is a wise woman."

"She is, and I always figured that keeping silent on the subject was her way to keep from telling me lies. Now I might ask her if my father's name is Arawn."

He shrugs, still looking pleased. "Better to hear it from her than from me." Taking hold of the kayak, he glances at me over his shoulder. "I won't ask you to cross the water with me, as it is not yet your time. There are men who depend on you, to whom you must return." He climbs into the single seat and shoves off with his paddle.

For a moment, I picture myself running after him and climbing into the boat. I could. I know that in my bones.

Those silver filaments grow even fainter.

Still, they're strong enough to make my choice an obvious one. "Thank you, Arawn of Annwn. It's not yet my—"

My words are cut short when the world around me jerks like a single shudder of a 9.0 earthquake. When I regain my balance, I'm back on the beach. It's dark, the moon overhead a slender sliver of light. The place smells of chemicals and smoke and as far as I can tell, the beach is deserted except for police tape blowing in the steady breeze.

Hugging myself against the chill, I start to walk.

CHAPTER THIRTY-THREE

DAVID

This is the part where I want to say, *And they lived happily ever after.*

I can't say that, though. Not yet.

In my bones I believe Connor will come back to us. Sitting in that hotel room with its weird orange wall, I'm having trouble connecting my bones to my conscious thought.

And Trajan? He's not connected to anything at all.

I'm on one bed, he's on the other. Normally I'd try to babble my way into cheering him up. Not tonight. His stare is so distant I'm not sure we're in the same universe.

I mean, he's been through a lot. I picked up some scuttlebutt from Sheena and Brodie. He'd claimed a new level of authority by turning a human, but the dude he'd turned ended up being staked, likely by one of Betancourt's minions. In turn, he'd staked his maker, the kind of action that has to have an emotional price tag.

You don't know what something like that is going to cost until you have to pay the bill.

And in the middle of everything, Connor goes up in smoke. Or at least he did a good impression of it. If I close my eyes, I can see the firebomb on repeat. My gut hurts, my body aches, and I desperately need a shower.

But I can't leave Trajan alone.

"How did you get rid of the elves?"

I startle so hard I all but levitate. "Um, what?"

"The elves. Why didn't they follow us back here, demanding the Princess's body?"

It's a good question. I reach back for who did what, when and try to come up with an answer. "I believe Sheena told them to fuck off."

There's a pause before he answers. "And they did?"

"Maybe?"

"How much longer till sunrise?"

I check my phone. The weather app gives me a precise answer. "Forty-seven minutes."

"Because they might try to break in and stake me in retaliation."

Shit. Hadn't thought of that. "Abby and Cliffe went back to Sheena's. I guess they could help me stand guard." No way could I stay awake all day.

Not after the night we'd had. "Or maybe I can track down Marcus."

My cousin booked a separate hotel room, making noise about moving to LA permanently. *File under: Deal with later.*

"No. We need to reach out to them somehow and negotiate a truce. I can't spend the rest of my…life waiting for an elf to strike."

I chew on that for a minute. "Elves are such assholes."

His expression doesn't change but I sense a weak attempt at a laugh. "Of course," he says, "Connor's the one who knows how to get in touch with them."

Knows? Knew? Getting lost in the verb tenses helps me deflect the pain. "Then we'll ask him when he gets back."

Two can play that game.

It's been a good three hours since the debacle on the beach, and here we are, back to where we started. Me 'n' Trajan, alone. I'm really not ready for our experiment in polyamory to end, but if it has, then we need to lay the groundwork for the future. With that in mind, I crawl off my bed and onto Trajan's. He shifts, still staring at nothing, and I curl up next to him. Pack calls to pack.

I'm naked because I threw the clothes I'd been given at Betancourt's house into the first dumpster we passed, and I'm too foul to put anything clean on. Trajan's still in solid black, that one stubborn lock of hair falling into his face. "So, Tony, I guess we still have each other."

There's a long pause, and then he shifts again, draping an arm around my shoulders. "Sure, puppy. We still have each other and that's pretty damned good."

His voice is rough enough that I'm pretty sure he doesn't believe what he's saying. I don't poke it—*I am getting wise in my old age*—just curl in tighter. He's cool and he smells smokey. I relax, settling into the connection that's so much more than just emotion. Will I be able to shift without Connor? Right now, I'm too tired to care.

I'm almost asleep when someone knocks on the door. We both stare at it as if we think Kowalski and his gang are going to bust through any second. "The elves wouldn't knock, right?" *Asking for a friend...*

I'm the more mobile of the two of us, so I get up. I'll look through the peep hole and either it'll be a friend who won't care if I'm nude or a not-friend and I won't let them in.

I look through the peep hole, and relief hits me so hard my knees give way.

"Puppy? David? Who is it?"

Trajan reels himself in from never-neverland and gets to me in about three steps. I can't speak or I'll start to sob. He's trying to help me up and

I'm scrabbling at the doorknob and neither of us are having any success.

We're stopped by another knock. I flop back on my ass and manage to grind out, "Open it."

Connor MacPherson steps into the room.

Trajan's frozen in place, hands open to the air. I manage to scoot over to where Connor is standing, then crawl up his body like he's a tree.

It's him. Warm whiskey and leather. He wraps an arm around my waist and reaches in Trajan's direction.

Guido's staring like one of us is a ghost.

"*Mo shíorghrá*," Connor murmurs, and still Trajan doesn't move. Then he does, slamming the door shut hard. He takes Connor's hand. I reach for him and he takes a step closer.

"I thought you were gone again." Trajan's broken, his words laced with sadness.

Since Trajan's not coming any closer, Connor and I go to him.

"I told you I'm hard to kill." Connor doesn't smile, but there's warmth in his tone. "Although if you want me to leave, I'll understand. I do not deserve—"

"Shut that shit right down." I've got a finger pointed at Connor's face. "We are pack. You aren't going anywhere."

"I get that, David." Connor wraps his hand around my finger, gently moving it out of range of his eyeballs. "But Trajan has a right to expect better treatment from a lover than I've shown him so far."

"So far." I glare at them both. "Seems to me you've got time to make things better, then."

Connor gives us a guarded smile. "Trajan?"

The vampire heaves a sigh. "I have questions, but right now I think we're all too tired to answer them. Let's go to bed."

It's not the ringing endorsement I'd hoped for, but it's good enough for now. "Last one to the shower gets cold water."

Neither of them follow me, but I don't care. They need time together, even if they just sit there with their tongues tied. Sure enough, when I come out of the bathroom, they're in one of the beds, Trajan spooned behind Connor. I'm the little spoon in that arrangement, so I tuck myself in beside Connor and shut my eyes.

Turns out, Jacques Betancourt's demise has surprisingly few repercussions. Tatiana made peace with her family, so we no longer worry that raging elves will bother us in our sleep. Delia Packard claimed a large chunk of Betancourt's real estate and other properties as restitution for the murder of her scion. The rest was divided up between the other area sires.

Except for the house in the Bird streets in Beverly Hills.

Madame Packard gave that to Trajan.

We're here, at least temporarily, and while we all hope that particular adventure is over, Trajan wants us to watch for a vampire he saw at the bonfire, one with ties to Delia Packard.

I know the vamp he means. Can a vampire be a warlock as well? Someone was helping Jacques find power, but we can answer that question when it jumps up to bite us. Hopefully not for a long while. This house, with its swimming pool and the view of forever, is too nice to let worry in.

Besides, we need the space. Abby's still around, bitching about how I'm not her alpha, I'm her brother. She and Cliffe share a room downstairs, which gives us a little privacy, at least. They're like, besties, and every so often they go out for a night on the town and I shudder at the stories they tell the next day. Being the older brother is hard.

Marcus and I are rebuilding our friendship in tiny little baby steps. He wants to be part of our pack, and so far I've moved from bad to neutral on the idea.

Trajan, Connor, and I can't have sex anywhere, anytime anymore, but group homes are kind of a wolf thing.

"Hey, what time is it?" I shout the question, most of my attention on the garlic I'm mincing. Abby and Cliffe are drinking wine and coaching my cooking technique from the kitchen's center island.

"Six forty-five," Cliffe says, pouring herself another glass.

"Should you be cooking garlic?" Abby's smirk says she's teasing. "I mean, vampire and all."

I smirk right back at her. "Old wives' tale, doll."

"I don't mind garlic." Trajan gets everyone's attention. He's leaning in the doorway, wearing a pair of track pants and —

"Your goddamn Mickey Mouse tee shirt," I squeal. "Haven't seen that one in way too long."

My hit-man vampire's all cute and sexy, hair messy, bulgy muscles bulging. "It's the only thing that's clean," he says, and I sashay over for a quick kiss.

"I ran the washer this afternoon." I shrug and return to my garlic. I still haven't figured out what I'm going to do with my life, but for now, I'm happily making pasta with meat sauce and a big Caesar salad. Connor should be here soon, and I expect Marcus to join us, as well.

Trajan pours himself a shot of tequila. He leans against the island and even though I've got my back to him, I can feel the weight of his gaze. "Stop looking at my ass." I stick my booty out to give him a better view.

"You love it," he says, and I laugh some more, because I do.

"Ew." Abby and Cliffe make faces. I ignore them. They move on to debating which podcast to listen to—they're both true crime addicts—while I brown meat and steal glances at Trajan.

Connor and Marcus arrive at about the same time. I give Connor a kiss and give Marcus a smile and holler, "Plating! Everybody wash your hands and come to supper."

They do and we sit down together. The dining room has a sideways view of the city lights and the conversation tumbles along. Connor shares tales of murder and mayhem and Marcus talks about his plan to return to Seattle to pack up our stuff. Ours. Mine and his. I guess we're Angelenos now.

As soon as Connor's done eating, I hop up, not even bothering to make an excuse for why he and Trajan need to come upstairs with me.

The others can clear the table.

We settle in Connor's room. It doesn't take much to get Connor out of his business clothes and even less time to make me naked. Trajan strips off his tee shirt—*can't get naughty with Mickey*—and stretches out across the bed. Connor joins him, and I work my way in between them. I kneel there, vampire cock in one hand, Danaan cock in the other.

"This is good. This right here." I stroke them, happy to be making my men happy.

"You're good," Trajan says, his dark eyes heavy with lust.

Connor wraps his hand around mine, guiding my stroke. "We're good."

We're good, and I'm glad. We've still got stuff, but we've also got time. Time, and our unconventional pack, and our love. None of us have ever said that word, but it's there in the connection we share, in our touch, in our hearts.

We're right where we need to be.

About the Author

Liv Rancourt is a multi-published author of m/m romance. Because love is love, even with fangs.

Liv likes to write stories about vampires, either contemporary or historical. Sometimes she branches out into other paranormal realms, but there's always magic, and there's always romance. She also co-authors two m/m paranormal romance series with Irene Preston. Their partnership works because Liv is good at blowing things up and Irene is good at explaining why.

When Liv isn't writing she takes care of tiny premature babies in the NICU. Her husband is a soul of patience, her kids are her pride and joy, and her cat Praline (pronounced PRAH-leen) is endlessly entertaining. Happy reading!